I0787969

BIOGRAPHY

H A Howe is a writer and lyricist. *Every Picture Inspires A Story* is her third collection of short stories. She has also written various plays, and one of her earlier ones, an historical play, was translated into French and German and the performance rights have been licensed for production in three countries, and is being developed as a feature film. If you want to contact the author, you can email her on h-a-howe@h-a-howe.com

Many of H A Howe's songs have been published in 29 countries worldwide. A small selection of her lyrics can be found on her website www.h-a-howe.com.

PRAISE FOR H A HOWE'S PREVIOUS WORKS

"Neat as a knitting pattern; dark as a closed coffin." I think captures Howe's special style.
Mike Hodges, writer/director: "Get Carter", "Flash Gordon"

"I wasn't surprised to hear that the author H A Howe was also a lyricist because a lyric writer's job is to eliminate the unnecessary, to never meander, be as economic as possible and illuminate character. In her first book *Short Stories* this is exactly what she does so effectively. I must start listening to her songs."
Don Black, OBE, lyricist (Oscar winner, "Diamonds Are Forever", "Man With the Golden Gun", numerous musicals & films)

"Mrs. Howe's chief asset is a capacity to draw the reader in to her tales, making the reader eager to know what happens next..."
Herbert Kretzmer OBE, journalist, lyricist (wrote the words to the musical Les Miserables)

"Ms. Howe's second book of short stories, *More Thorns Than Roses*, certainly lives up to its title. It is definitely thorny, edgy, dark, and very eloquently written. The tales ring true and leave you wanting more as soon as possible. She is a very gifted writer."
Peter Bogdanovich, film director/writer/critic/ film historian ("The Last Picture Show", "Paper Moon", "Mask")

"Short stories doesn't quite say it. H A Howe's tales of misadventure are as brief as a moment and as fully formed as a thriller."
John Nathan, journalist – The Times/The Independent/Jewish Chronicle

There are precious few collections of short stories around at the moment - … quite often all you want is to get involved with the characters just long enough to read about just one episode in their lives. Hugely enjoyable collection by H A Howe – I can't recommend it highly enough.
Book Monthly

More Thorns Than Roses is a remarkable collection of short stories from H A Howe. It's an interesting collection of disparate ideas and themes. It's light and frothy, yet it is also tart and salty. It's as if someone has made a really rather splendidly fluffy meringue and replaced half of the caster sugar with some crunchy pink Himalayan salt.

There are tales of love, of betrayal, of fears, real and imagined and tragedy events of the kind that make people shake their heads and say: "We should have seen that coming" but, somehow, nobody ever does.

There's guilt, sometimes where there should be none, and an absence of guilt where guilt should be a crushing remorse.

There are cruelties upon cruelties and acts of stupidity, thoughtlessness and of fecklessness.

Yet there are also moments of great tenderness, of love, and of sacrifice and of hope. And of situations that are beyond all realistic hope. And, finally, of light.
That's Books and Entertainment Book Shop

Every Picture Inspires A Story

H A Howe

Copyright © 2017 H A Howe

The moral right of the author has been asserted.

Apart from any fair dealing for the purposes of research or private study, or criticism
or review, as permitted under the Copyright, Designs and Patents Act 1988,
this publication may only be reproduced, stored or transmitted, in any form
or by any means, with the prior permission in writing of the publishers,
or in the case of reprographic reproduction in accordance with
the terms of licenses issued by the Copyright Licensing Agency.
Enquiries concerning reproduction outside those terms should be sent to the publishers.

Every Picture Inspires A Story by H A Howe is a work of fiction, any resemblance
between characters and actual persons, living or dead, is coincidental.

Victory Entertainment Ltd
52 Lancaster Road
London N4 4PR
victoryentertainment@btconnect.com

ISBN 978-0-9929069-4-8

British Library Cataloguing in Publication Data.
A catalogue record for this book is available from the British Library.

Cover design: Patrick Shart
Editorial services: Jess Bancroft

"Logic will get you from A to Z;
imagination will get you everywhere."
Albert Einstein

CONTENTS

Every Picture Inspires A Story

David Hockney — *Pool and Steps, Le Nid du Duc,* 1971
Acrylic on canvas 72 × 72" © David Hockney

Pool and Steps

'Why on earth would you want to sell this,' he greeted the figure awaiting him as he jumped out of his car. He had been in the real estate business for ten years and had managed to shift some pretty amazing properties, but this one took his breath away. Barely noticeable from the road, but the moment the big iron gates opened to allow him access, he knew he was entering Paradise. His top of the range Ferrari shrank to insignificance as it climbed the gently ascending driveway to reach its destination. Although he was only able to glimpse part of the land surrounding the main building as he passed through, it did not escape his attention that everything was exquisitely designed and kept in immaculate condition – the orchard, the various pools, the waterfall – an earthly Garden of Eden.

He stopped in front of the magnificent mansion even though the driveway continued round the back of the property. The house, he barely dared refer to it as such as the term seemed far too belittling for this imposing construction, reminded him of a fortress. Yes, an exquisite modern castle! If King Arthur were alive today, that's what he would have had erected for himself.

She stood there like a statue draped in silk. A faint smile was all he received in response to his question.

'Sorry, I was totally taken in by the stunning beauty of it all,' he said apologetically, whilst extending his hand, 'Mark Norton. Mrs Weiland, I assume?'

She did not take his hand, nor did she confirm that she was the proprietor who had asked him to value the property. Her demeanour immediately diminished any hope he had had of being offered some refreshment before inspecting this extensive property in the scorching California sun. Her stony reception made him even more conscious of the heat and he could feel his mouth drying out. He always liked chatting to his clients - to put them at ease, gain their trust; and ideally to find out their reason for selling – were they moving abroad, did they have money problems, were they looking for a quick sale; but also to establish the personality of the place. This client, however, seemed completely content cocooned in enigma. He wanted to have this mansion on his books, but it would be hard work to get it.

'Have you lived here long?' he ventured.

'Is that important?' she asked in a tone that made him think of a glass full of ice and reminded him how hot and parched he was.

He longed to leave the terrace and move inside where the air conditioning would make him feel more comfortable, but he had to wait for her to suggest it.

'Buyers generally want to know all sorts of things about a property and the people who live in it,' he answered matter-of-factly, trying to reassure her that he wasn't just making small talk or being nosy without a purpose, but that his interest was purely professional.

'You can tell them whatever you like.'

'I can't just make up a story.'

'You have my permission.'

Her non-committal responses started to annoy him because they were gnawing away at his confidence. In his desperation to make conversation, to maybe discover some relevant detail, he nearly asked the one question that should never be asked 'Do you live here alone?' It is a question reserved for con-men and makes sellers immediately suspicious, with the result of them wanting to get rid of you as quickly as possible. He was good at his job, his success was proof of that, and he was a master at administering all the bullshit necessary to sway the client in his favour. Normally, he would have been sitting down by now discussing his fees over a nice cold drink. This case needed a different approach. And he had yet to find the right one.

'It really is a spectacular property, so unique,' he beamed, in an attempt to overcome his growing discomfort and onset of embarrassment about the beads of sweat multiplying on his forehead. It didn't help that she seemed totally unaffected by the rising temperature as this late morning in the middle of August crept slowly towards midday.

'I know,' she replied sharply as if she was about to lose her patience with him for stating the obvious. He knew he had to change direction if he was ever going to get her approval. Flattery was no way forward here.

'Would it be alright to have a look around?'

'That's what you are here for.'

'Will you show me around?'

'I'll walk with you through the main building. You can do the gardens and outbuildings yourself – nothing's locked.'

He took out his i-pad. 'Is it ok to take notes as we walk around?'

She raised her eyebrows in demonstration of how stupid she thought the question was. 'It would be advisable. As you might have noticed, it is a big estate.'

'Photos? Can I take photos?'

'Snap away.'

He followed her along the large terrace, grateful to be finally walking into some shade thrown by the magnificent palm trees that were lining the path. She floated across the marble floor towards the interior. In front of them, glass doors he hadn't even realised were there, slid open automatically to give access to an enormous atrium. 'How many rooms are there,' he asked.

'Twenty-two bedrooms upstairs, various rooms on the ground floor. A kitchen somewhere over there,' she gestured vaguely to the right as if she'd never been there.

The interior was everything the outside had promised and more. The most up-to-date hi-tech innovations were incorporated into every room. The décor throughout was extravagant but stylish and, despite a lavish display of extraordinary features, felt unimposing and almost minimalistic due to the generous size of each room, and with there never being more than one focal point in a room. All rooms were en-suite, all offered a unique design. Some had a Jacuzzi in the middle, others were fitted with Japanese water features. There were winter gardens with an array of exotic flora and astonishingly rare examples of taxidermy. The most notable was the majestic elephant bull in the Indian inspired suite, placed in front of a hand painted mural depicting its natural habitat. The viewing, during which not a word was exchanged between them, took a good two hours, and yet he felt rushed. She seemed to hurry him along – every time they entered a room and he'd start his notes or to take photographs, she would immediately move ahead of him to the next room where she'd wait for him impatiently. Still, the viewing went smoothly and business-like. It would be such an easy sale, and a very lucrative one.

So far, there had not been any indication of another living thing in the entire place. Every room, including the master bedroom, looked deserted. Even if she didn't share the property with anybody, he knew that it would take a considerable workforce of cleaners and gardeners to keep it as impeccable as this. Yet, there was no sign of movement anywhere. It felt eerie, and as much as he wanted to become the sole selling agent for this place, he couldn't wait to step outside again. Even 40 degrees Celsius in the shade was preferable, less suffocating than this stifling emptiness. He followed her down the wide, winding staircase, taking in the vastness of the ground floor. Before he had reached the bottom stair, she'd turned round. 'How long will you take for the outside,' she asked.

'It depends how many out-buildings there are,' he replied smilingly, disguising how taken aback he was by her abrupt manner. He was about to ask her for a glass of water, but changed his mind as he didn't think she would appreciate such liberty. Instead he said, 'Have you already moved out?'

'I'm about to,' she answered without seeming to take objection to the question.

Encouraged by her relaxed tone, he ventured, 'Where will you go?'

'Away,' came the off-hand reply, as if she was already regretting having allowed herself to be dragged into a personal conversation.

'Well … erm …,' he retracted, 'wherever you are moving to, it couldn't possibly be like this.'

'I hope not,' she replied calmly, and he was convinced that he saw a fleeting smile move across her pale, flawless complexion. She briefly closed her eyes as if to remind herself of the task in hand. 'There are 6 cottages, 3 garages, a couple of sheds,' she informed him. 'You can take one of the golf buggies at the back of the house … quicker to get around.'

He considered this for a few seconds before replying, 'Shouldn't take me longer than a couple of hours.'

'The cottages are basically identical so … really you'd need only have a look at one. Same with the garages. Except,' she hesitated, 'I would be happy to sell the cars with the estate. And there's really nothing special about the sheds. So shall we say … an hour, hour and a half max?'

He didn't like being rushed, he might overlook some important detail that could result in a potential sale falling through, but he didn't feel that he could argue this point. 'Of course, I shall try my very best,' he agreed politely.

He had already reached the point where the glass doors opened magically, exposing him to a light tropical breeze that made his face burn and announced the renewal of sweat patches under his beige linen jacket, when she suddenly called after him, 'Wait! You mustn't touch anything … especially not by the main pool area … in fact,' she was now walking towards him and for the first time he sensed some anxiety in her voice, 'don't go anywhere near the main pool. You can have a look at a later stage when it's been cleaned up. … Oh, and there's a bottle of water in the buggy, in case you are thirsty.'

He nodded, and with a cheerful 'Thank you,' he made his way to claim one of ten golf buggies that were lining the entrance to a full-sized golf course a mere five minutes from the main building yet hidden from sight by a row of cypresses. It was easy to navigate his way around the grounds, and the immaculate state throughout made light work of his inspection. Regardless of her request, he was determined to at least have a peek at the main pool. It was totally hidden from sight, unable to be seen even from the main house, but he had an idea where it would be.

He had finished well in time so he left the buggy parked at the cottage nearest the pool and climbed up the winding path until he reached a platform surrounded by cast iron railings. This offered a magnificent vantage point from which to overlook most of the grounds. At the other end of the plateau was a descending staircase which he was convinced would lead to the pool. After every five to ten steps there was another 'look-out' area but it wasn't until the second flight of stairs that he was able to glimpse a patch of radiant blue water still quite some distance beneath him. Every platform he reached exposed a little more of the pool, like adding pieces to a jigsaw puzzle, until he was finally confronted with an Olympic sized pool, it's water splashing silently over the edges as if secretly trying to escape its marble entrapment. The surrounding high walls from which waterfalls descended guaranteed absolute privacy. He imagined her swimming here in the nude - a thought made all the more vivid by the bathrobe that had carelessly been left lying on the marble tiles. When, a second later, he discovered the leather sandals, male sandals, a different thought entered his mind – somebody might actually be in the pool house, and that's why she didn't want him to come here. He was about to turn round and hasten back when he spotted a pair of feet peeking out from behind a bush. Deciding that he might as well make his presence known and deal with the consequences of his disobedience, rather than making matters worse by sneaking away when he might already have been found out, he shouted, 'Hello! So sorry to disturb you,' as he started walking towards the outstretched body. The man was lying motionless in a pool of blood, naked, a large knife stuck in the side of his neck, his back showing multiple stab wounds.

He raced up the stairs and back to the cottage where he had parked the golf buggy, not caring that his shirt was sticking to him underneath his jacket, not worried that she might be watching him. He wasn't really able to focus on anything other than wondering whether she had killed the man or not. There was a possibility that she didn't even know about the body being there, but he doubted that. He should have called the police immediately yet, for some weird reason, he wanted to see her first. She was waiting for him by the entrance of the golf course.

'You saw him, didn't you,' she said calmly. 'I told you not to go there.'

'Did you ...?'

'Does it matter?' she asked, seemingly surprised by his question.

He was taken aback by her reaction and her relaxed attitude. In a way, he had to admit that it didn't really matter who the murderer was – a crime had been committed and should be reported, the rest was for the police to establish. Yet somehow, he needed to know if it had been her. If so, he figured, she must have had a good reason. She didn't strike him as a homicidal psychopath, not that he had any reason to believe that he would recognise one. 'Have you reported it?,' he finally asked.

'Not yet. Have you?'

'Not yet. I wasn't sure if you even knew ... so I thought I'd tell you first.'

'I wanted to wait until you'd finished your viewing before ringing the police. There's no urgency really ... he *is* dead. And I live here alone now so ... do you want some iced tea?'

The murdered body by the pool, one person living in a place big enough to accommodate a hundred, her calmness - the whole situation seemed so surreal, and yet somehow he could see nothing wrong with having a drink, now that it was finally being offered. 'Something stronger would be good,' he replied. 'Any chance of a gin and tonic?'

'Of course,' she smiled graciously. 'I might join you.'

They sat outside on the shaded veranda sipping their ice cold drinks as if it was the most normal thing on earth. For a long time they remained seated opposite each other in total stillness, both of them wondering how to proceed. She had everything worked out; she just needed to decide how much to tell him. As for Mark, he just wanted some answers, but he knew he had to be careful in the way he phrased his questions.

'He was my husband,' she suddenly broke the silence. 'I'm sure you've wondered.'

'Yeah,' he replied slowly, 'about that and other things.' He looked at her intensely as he asked, 'Did you kill him?'

She didn't flinch or avert his gaze. 'It's not a simple yes or no answer.'

'I have time. As you said, there's no hurry.'

'But I'll have a lot of explaining to do once the police get here, and I'm not sure I need a dress rehearsal.'

Every time she volunteered some information, she seemed to immediately backtrack. Was it just that she didn't trust him or did she really have that much to hide?

'What's your first name?' he asked, more harshly than he intended to, when it was only meant as an attempt to loosen up the increasingly tense atmosphere.

She smiled at him, the same all-knowing, slightly bored smile he'd seen her display earlier. 'Lily,' she said.

'Well, Lily, I'm Mark. I would love to sell your property regardless of the circumstances. But, considering that somebody has been stabbed to death by your swimming pool, I assume there will be a certain amount of press coverage, and I would like to have some prior knowledge of what to expect.' He then added, as a way of diffusing the sarcasm he had adopted, 'After all, I have to reassure the potential buyer that the place is safe … that it doesn't belong to a mafia boss or warlord … or that the murder isn't due to a break-in. So, anything you could share with me?'

'It was purely domestic. A very private matter. Hopefully the press won't make too much of it.'

'So you did kill him?'

'I didn't say that.'

'Ok, what are you going to tell the police?'

'The truth.'

Mark had had enough of her evasive answers. He was losing his temper and was not worried anymore about showing it because one thing was for sure – she would not get another agent interested in selling the estate until all this mess was sorted out. It could be weeks before the police would allow anybody on the premises again.

'Right,' he said sharply, 'you have to give me something, otherwise you'd better call another realtor because I'll be leaving right now, and I'll call the police on my way out.'

She closed her eyes and inhaled deeply. 'Let me top up our drinks first.'

She had barely set down the full glasses when she started. 'My husband bought this place five years ago, with my money – I come from a very wealthy family, you know. Once we'd moved in, he became tyrannical and abusive.' She paused whilst searching his face for a reaction. When she got none, she took a sip from her drink before carrying on. 'I tried to leave him a couple of times, but never got very far before he found me. In the end, I decided it wasn't worth the black eyes and bruises, so I started to accept my fate.'

'Why didn't you go to the police,' Mark asked in a tone void of sympathy, and hinting heavily that he was not convinced by her story.

'My money made him a very powerful man,' she replied and, ignoring Mark's raised eyebrows and cynical grin, continued, 'on my 30th birthday, he'd planned a surprise trip. I was already surprised that he'd even remembered it, having not acknowledged my three previous birthdays, but the real surprise was yet to come. We ended up on a remote island somewhere in Indonesia in an even remoter beach house where he had paid three locals to rape me whilst he went for a walk on the beach.'

She had started to breathe more heavily and Mark noticed that her hand was shaking slightly as she reached for her drink. He could see no reason anymore not to believe her, but nor was there any doubt in his mind that she had killed her husband. Yet, he could not look on the deed as a criminal act, only as an act of justice. 'If you go to the police,' he started slowly, 'you will be put on trial, and even if you get a very sympathetic judge, you could still go to prison.'

'This was prison,' she whispered as she let her eyes glide over her surroundings. 'Anyway, there's nothing else to be done. The moment you leave, I shall call the police. I have already prepared a written statement. I would like you to draw up some papers for the sale of the property.

I give you full authority, and I agree to any fee you find fit to charge for your service.'

'Did your husband have any enemies?'

'A fair amount,' she said hesitantly, looking at him questioningly, … 'he wasn't just unpleasant to me … and his favourite hobby was to make people financially dependent on him.'

'So lots of people will be pleased that he is dead?'

'I guess so,' she said smiling but puzzled. 'You think this might help my case?'

'I'm just saying that you are not necessarily the most obvious killer. Somebody else may have had enough of him. And this is a big place, it's possible that you hadn't even discovered him until now … with me, for instance, when you showed me round.'

'What are you implying?'

'That you shouldn't take the wrap for it, it's not fair … not after what you've been through.'

She sat there in silence for a couple of minutes, considering what he'd said. 'But if the police find out that I'm lying, my case will look a lot worse. I don't think I should risk it.'

Knowing of course that she was absolutely right, he thought it over before offering his help. Having established that she stabbed her husband only a couple of hours before he arrived at the property, he suggested he could be her alibi, that he could write a statement saying that he'd arrived earlier and was with her whilst the murder must have taken place. She was immensely touched by this gesture and swore repeatedly that nobody had ever shown her such kindness.

'But,' she added shyly, 'what if you change your mind?'

'I wouldn't,' he said resolutely. 'You can trust me. In fact,' he opened his i-pad, 'I'll change the appointment time in my diary right now.'

'You would really do that for me?' she asked seemingly moved by his offer.

'Done. The bastard got what he deserved, as far as I'm concerned.'

'Oh no, it won't work! The knife,' she stuttered … 'it's mine, it's got my fingerprints on it.'

'We can wipe the knife.'

'No, that won't do. It is my knife - everybody knows I keep it in my desk. It was a gift from my father – an African hunting knife.'

Mark pondered on this for a second. 'Ok, I'll take the knife and dispose of it, and I'll get rid of it some distance from here. I'll do it now.'

She thanked him over and over again, and the fading murmurs of her gratitude 'Such risk … nobody's ever been so kind to me' followed him echo-like as he walked away to retrieve the golf buggy. He hurried down to the swimming pool. All the blood had dried up and there was a colony of ants crawling on and around the body. The knife came out more easily than he expected, the surprise of which made him stagger backwards. The blade was covered in congealed blood. He quickly put it in the plastic bag, but some residue of blood was left stuck on his sweaty palm. He walked to the side of the pool and knelt down. But as he immersed his hand in the cool water, he suddenly noticed the appearance of a large shadow rising from behind him. He turned around to find himself surrounded by five grim looking policemen. 'Get up,' one of them demanded sharply. And before he could even protest, he was handcuffed and told his rights. Only as he was being led away, did he see Lily kneeling next to the body, sobbing her heart out.

The realisation that she had set him up came as soon as one of the policemen picked up the bag containing the knife with his fingerprints all over it. It turned out that it wasn't a special knife at all – just a fancy steak knife, and there were at least twenty more of them in a cupboard by the barbecue area. She had planned it well, and acted it skilfully – from her haughtiness on his arrival to the victim of marital abuse – he had been totally convinced by her performance. And he would never know if there was any truth in even a single word she'd uttered.

Pieter Breugel the Elder
The Peasant Wedding, 1567

The Peasant Wedding

'More wine!' demanded Jorgen, holding out his cup. 'I'll not go thirsty on my wedding day!'

'Do you ever?' shouted Vincent, the groom's cousin, to the amusement of the jolly company. 'Your bride seems none too happy about it though. Better make sure she gets what's due to her tonight!'

'Ay, to be sure, there'll be no complaints,' Jorgen nodded in his wife's direction and then turned to wink at Vincent. 'She'll be smiling tomorrow.'

Grete did not look at her husband or indeed anybody else in the barn. She continued to keep her eyes downcast and, while everybody else took advantage of the ample offerings of food and drink, Grete chose to abstain from both. Determined to block out her surroundings, she appeared to be intensely concentrating as if there, beyond the noise and spectacle, she was hoping to get a glimpse of a brighter future, of a different destiny. It was her wedding, but she did not feel part of it. The man opposite her – a stranger, now her husband. The raucous guests – his friends, but unfamiliar to her. Her only relation present was her father, and she felt more distant from him right now than ever before. She was vaguely aware of the old man sitting somewhere to her left as she heard snatches of some lewd jokes followed by his fake laughter, attempting to lower himself to his guests' level of entertainment, pretending to fit in. Tomorrow, he would resume his normal life as a wealthy farmer and their employer, whilst she …

Grete was in love once, really in love, when she was young and pretty, with a dashing young lad, the son of a landowner, set to inherit his father's holding. He swore he loved her too, but then left to see the world and never returned. As the years went by, her father grew more and more anxious to find someone to take over the farm but, once his daughter had finally got over her lost love, there were no more suitors. It was a big farm, and her father was finding it increasingly hard to keep control over it all. Grete did what she could but somehow the workers preferred to take commands from men. Jorgen was a good worker and the people listened to him. He had worked for her father since he was twelve years old. He had known her mother, and he had known Grete since she was born. It was Jorgen who lifted her onto her first pony when she was but a little lass. And it was Jorgen who ran to fetch the doctor when her mother battled with her life giving birth to Grete's brother. For a long time, Grete blamed Jorgen for her mother's and baby brother's death; for not running fast enough, believing they would have survived had the doctor arrived sooner. She was only five then.

Three years ago, Mr Boorman promoted Jorgen to farm supervisor. As a way of celebration, Jorgen was invited to lunch with them at their residence. It was the first, and only time Jorgen had been in their formal dining room. He arrived with an expression of torture which remained on his face throughout the meal. His freshly starched shirt seemed too tight around the collar. It was his Sunday best, yet, when he could no longer hide his arms in his lap, its shabbiness became embarrassingly obvious. And when his rough, coarse hands groped for the silver fork, Grete almost couldn't bear it. He looked grotesque amongst the fine silver, the delicate glass goblets. To invite him to a formal lunch had been a mistake - to give him more responsibility on the farm, had not. Jorgen's daily work load did not change, but giving him greater authority meant that he could tend to problems without worrying old Mr Boorman. Jorgen was liked and respected by all the other workers. He was one of them, and he felt comfortable amongst them. Grete had hardly ever spoken to him in all these years. She was aware of him, no more; just as she was aware of the stable boy, the shepherds, the milkmaids.

A couple of months ago, Mr Boorman had to take to his bed, having caught a chill. Recovery was slow. When he finally felt well enough to get up, he summoned his daughter and declared, 'I have offered Jorgen the farm … providing he'll take you as his wife.'

'No!' She had shouted her unwillingness with the same fierceness and stubbornness that she had displayed when she was a weeny girl. Like the time she had taken objection to her father making her walk home from the market instead of letting her sit on the wagon next to him, just because she had annoyed him during the day. She had cried, stamped her foot, thrown stones at the wagon. But walk she did.

'It is settled,' he replied sharply, 'the wedding is in two weeks.'

Devastated and furious, but utterly helpless against her father's will, Grete had stormed off. As she'd crossed the courtyard, Jorgen, tending to a hole in the chicken enclosure, had looked up briefly and nodded shyly in her direction. That was the only contact she had had with him since the unfortunate lunch. Yes, he had been around all her life, but they had lived in parallel universes, and neither had ever crossed into the other's world. Now they were supposed to merge – he uncomfortable in her surroundings, she loathing his.

The sudden touch of Jorgen's hand on her shoulder made her jump. She had not noticed that he had left his seat opposite her. He bent down and his hoarse voice whispered in her ear, 'It is time, Grete. Come.' She got up slowly, uncertain. When he noticed her trembling body, he added gently, 'They're alright really, my lot, just take some getting used to.'

She raised her head, ready to face his coarseness, and, for the first time ever, she looked into his eyes, expecting to find them blurred and bloodshot. Instead, she saw only honesty and goodness, and a gentleness that she had not thought him capable of. He held out his hand and, with the flicker of a smile, she accepted it.

Honoré Daumier
The Pleading Lawyer (Un Avocat Plaidant), 1845

The Pleading Lawyer

'So, Mr Burden, I ask you: do you plead guilty to the charges brought against you? Have you committed the crime you are accused of? Mr Burden, are you guilty?' the prosecutor asked for the second time. But Jim Burden found himself unable to answer. The question had tortured him for weeks. Was he guilty? How was he supposed to answer truthfully, under oath, when he had yet to judge himself?

It wasn't a question of punishment because that was dependent on jury and judge. This was a matter of conscience and morality. Was he responsible for what had happened? Did he consider *himself* guilty?

Liza was a naughty child, always mischievous, always disobedient. To tell her not to do something was like an invitation to do that very thing; to forbid her anything served merely as encouragement to attempt the strictly prohibited. Aged five, Liza already proved a tremendous challenge for her parents; at the age of thirteen, they were unable to cope with her. Liza would come and go as it suited her, she did not help her parents look after their modest farm, she was not interested in schooling - she'd simply do as she pleased. She was argumentative, inappropriately promiscuous for her age, and she was very rude, to her parents and to anybody who'd try to tell her anything she did not want to hear. There was no disciplining her. Old Father Preston who had been begged by Liza's mother to appeal to their child's conscience, was given such a mouthful of abuse that he recommended exorcism as the only possibility to save their child from the abyss. Mrs Nolan endured daily agonies as she worried about her daughter's safety, and feared for her soul.

The first time Jim Burden saw Liza she was lying naked by the lake in the woods. He didn't know she was there, he just stumbled upon her on his way to take his daily bath in the lake. He was so shocked at the sight of another human being on what he considered his territory, and at such late hour, that he hadn't even noticed at first that she wasn't wearing any clothes. He only realised when she got up and approached him, void of any embarrassment. 'I've been waiting for you,' she said in a thin, high-pitched, child-like voice that bore a stark contrast to her fully formed womanly body. 'You come here to bathe at night, and sometimes you catch a fish for supper. Aren't you afraid here at night, all on your own?'

'No,' he replied, 'Aren't you afraid?'

'I'm not on my own. You are here.'

This made him smile. 'You are not frightened of me, then,' he asked, 'like most people in the village?'

'You must teach me how to catch fish with my bare hands.'

'It's luck, rather than skill,' he answered in a kinder tone.

'Then show me how to increase my luck because I've tried but haven't been successful. Although once I got my hands round one, quite a big one too, but the slippery bugger was so fast that it glided right through my fingers and disappeared between my legs.'

'Your hands are too small, and your feet probably too unsteady. Come back in five years when you're grown up,' he said more gruffly than he meant it. He wasn't used to talking to people, and he did not appreciate her intrusion into his routine.

Barely two feet away from him, she suddenly started to stroke and knead her breasts. 'I'll let you touch me if you help me catch one,' she whispered.

She was a child, naive and simple, but with an inbred instinct for sexuality. Jim Burden was not tempted by her offer, not even slightly aroused by it. He was 35 and had not thought of the 13 year old Liza as anything but a wayward, ill-disciplined youngster. It was the first time in years anybody from the village had ventured to his part of the forest. He sometimes saw the mayor and his hunting party chasing foxes at the other side of the lake, but they never came anywhere near his little plot. He would watch them occasionally, and take great delight when, at times, they were outwitted by their prey, but he always made sure to stay well hidden from their sight. People didn't like him, and he didn't like them. That's how it had been now for many years, ever since his wife had left him for the police inspector. And to justify their adultery, the two of them had painted him as a madman and a violent monster who had forced his wife into marrying him. They had even concocted a tale whereby the police inspector had rescued her from her husband's obscenities and murderous threats. Nobody believed his side of the story against the account of one of the village's most respected citizens. After that, life in the village became unbearable so he withdrew into the forest and became a total recluse. But at least he was self-sufficient, and he didn't have to listen to the tales of horror the villagers were making up about him.

'Put some clothes on,' he commanded.

'Why,' she screeched, outraged at his demand. 'I hate clothes – they make me itch and sweat, and they are all too tight … up here,' she cupped her breasts in her hands to demonstrate.'

Adopting a gentler tone, Jim replied, 'Because if other people saw you like this, they might get the wrong idea, and you might get hurt. Do your parents know that you are out this late?'

She shrugged her shoulders. 'Sometimes I don't go home at all.'

'And they don't mind?'

'In the beginning they did, but they are used to it by now. They say I'm possessed. Well, that's what the dirty old priest told them because I didn't let him put his stinking willie in my mouth anymore.'

Jim remembered Father Preston only too well – it was he who'd married him, and who, two years later, for a small reward, wrote off to the pope to request an annulment on the grounds that the bride was tricked into the marriage by devilish acts. Jim felt sorry for Liza.

He knew that sooner or later somebody would harm her. It saddened him that one so young should have such little chance of a happy life. But there was nothing he could do about it. He was also very aware of what would happen if anybody saw her with him, and he did not want to get into trouble. They had left him alone since he moved into the forest and he wanted to preserve his peace and quiet.

'You have to go now. And don't come back. I don't want you round here,' he said with exaggerated anger.

'I don't want to go, I like it here,' she replied sulkily. Then added indignantly, 'And you can't make me. I have as much right to bathe in this lake as you do.'

'I eat young girls,' he snapped threateningly. 'Didn't they tell you?'

He wasn't sure what reaction he had expected, but her bursting out laughing certainly took him by surprise. It was obvious that Liza wasn't scared of him, or indeed of anybody, which was worrying. As she insisted on hanging around his 'home,' he eventually agreed to teach her how to catch fish with her bare hands, providing she'd stay fully dressed.

She had managed to catch her first fish after just a couple of days but pretended it had slipped through her fingers again, although it was clear that she'd deliberately let it escape. So weeks went by, during which time Jim taught her to read a little, cook some simple dishes, and acquaint her with the names of the plants and trees in the forest. It was as happy a time either of them would ever have. Jim's gentle manner and laid back attitude combined with a diet of fresh fish, fruit and vegetables obviously agreed with Liza who seemed to be blossoming. Jim would insist though that Liza returned home at night to make sure her parents didn't worry. It was, however, a continuous struggle as Liza refused daily to obey. She'd even taken to begging him to allow her to stay. He remained adamant for a while, but then one day, when she rolled up the sleeves of her coarse shirt, he noticed the bruises on her arm. 'What happened to you,' he asked nodding in the direction of the bruises.

'Oh,' she shrugged her shoulders dismissively, 'The old man got carried away by passion.'

Jim didn't give it a further thought. Somehow he wasn't at all surprised that Liza would get a good hiding from her father every now and then, considering her stubbornness and rudeness. It was only later that evening, once it was dark, that he understood the full extent of her father's passion. It was just after supper and shortly before he would normally ask her to be heading home, when she drew close to him and started to unbutton her shirt, whispering, 'Shall I show you what the old man likes best?'

'No,' he shouted, and immediately distanced himself from her. But he did not send her away that night. He made up a bed for her in his make-shift cabin whilst he chose to sleep outside. He had become used to having company, and he had grown fond of Liza. He'd never realised how lonely he was before she arrived, but it was inconceivable for her to remain with him permanently. No good could come of it. He lay awake all night trying to find a solution. He didn't want to send her back home and have the abuse continue, but he didn't know what else to do. He got up early the next day and prepared a wholesome broth for breakfast before entering the cabin to wake her. When he came out again, he had a shotgun pointed in his face.

Liza's father lived up to Jim's expectations of him – he was a despicable and cruel man. Without uttering a word, Nick Nolan hit Jim across the head with the barrel of the rifle. The blow was so hard and unexpected that it made Jim stumble backwards against the wooden cabin wall with such a thump that Liza came running out in alarm. The moment she emerged, her father whacked her across the legs just as viciously, making her collapse to the floor and wince with pain. Jim pounced forward, but Nick Nolan shoved the barrel of his gun hard into Jim's stomach where it remained, unbolted. 'So this is your bastard's father,' he stated menacingly without averting his eyes from his target. It was a declaration, not a question.

'I never …,' Jim began to protest, but the pain of the barrel being shoved even harder into his stomach made him stop short.

'No,' cried Liza, 'I told you I'm not going to do it! I'm not covering up for you any more. It is your bastard that's growing inside me, no-one else's!'

Nick Nolan gave Jim another knock to the head before turning to Liza. 'You will say anything I tell you to when I'm finished with you,' he snarled whilst slamming the back of his rifle into her swollen abdomen. The moment Nolan started to focus his attention on Liza, Jim took advantage of being unobserved and hurried away. He was never able to answer, let alone justify to himself why he did. Why hadn't he just stayed and protected her? He could have fought. Even if he had died in the process, it would have been a less cowardly escape. But he'd panicked. Because he knew, that no matter what, he'd be the guilty one. Like last time. Nobody would believe his account of events, and his life would, once again, become a living hell. It had taken him years to overcome their abuse and insults, and his own anger at the injustice done him. He did not feel that he had the strength to go through all of that again. So he'd lost his nerve and ran. Had he thought about it clearly, he would have realised that there was no escape for him because, he was right, he would be blamed no matter what. But had he stayed, he might have been able to save Liza's life rather than standing trial for her murder. Nick Nolan had not managed to beat Liza into submission, so he beat her to death.

'Mr Burden,' the prosecutor shouted accompanied by re-enforcing gestures, 'Young Liza who you lured away from her distraught parents to live with you in the woods in sin, this innocent girl, carrying your unborn child … was battered to death outside your cabin! Mr Burden,' the prosecutor inflated his chest and settled into a more dignified pose before adapting a calm but stern tone, 'Isn't it true that, plagued by the consequences of her pregnancy and desperate to avoid trouble, you could only see one way out – to silence the girl. So, Mr Burden, let me ask you again: are you responsible for Liza Nolan's death? What do you plead? Guilty or not guilty?'

Jim Burden did blame himself for Liza's tragic end. He did feel responsible for her death, and he felt as guilty as if he had committed the vicious act himself; but most of all he felt ashamed, ashamed for running, for being a coward, for letting her down. He knew he would hang for her murder, regardless of his plea, and somehow he thought he deserved to. But he would not make it that easy for them. He would speak the truth before leaving this world even though he had little hope of being listened to, let alone believed.

'I am not guilty of the heinous crime you accuse me of, but I am guilty of not protecting Liza from her bestial father …,' At this the whole courtroom was in uproar and Jim struggled to make himself heard as he continued to shout out the truth at the top of his voice, '…who first impregnated her and then beat her to death because she refused to lie and blame her pregnancy on me. I hold myself responsible for her death, and I am prepared to die for my cowardice, but he is the one who committed a most despicable murder! It is *he* who slaughtered his own daughter! Do not doubt the words of a dying man, I have nothing to gain from lying. I shall face my lord with a truthful heart, but this monster of a man …'

Jim Burden, pointing vigorously at Nick Nolan, suddenly collapsed mid-sentence as a rifle shot silenced the courtroom. All eyes were on Nick Nolan and his raised shotgun. As Jim Burden sank dying to the ground he whispered, 'Now you'll hang.'

Francisco Goya
The Kite (La Cometa), 1777-1778

The Kite

'Come on,' she'd coaxed, 'head up high!' But his head was too heavy with sorrow and the many tears he had yet to shed. So, little Pedro continued trudging next to his mother, his chin firmly attached to his chest, whilst his tears left behind a sparkling trail as they trickled endlessly onto the dry sand.

'Look at the kite in the sky!' she'd suddenly called out and, without even realising, he had lifted his head and watched the colourful, rhombus-shaped face with its long tail dance above him to the rhythm of the wind. A moment later, his face had lit up as he laughed at the entertaining display. His mother smiled at having succeeded in lifting her son's head as well as his spirits. 'You see,' she'd said squeezing his little hand tighter, 'you have to keep your head up, no matter what – there might be a kite in the sky.'

That was a long time ago and he had no recollection of what had upset him so at the time. But he had never forgotten how lifting up his head, had also lifted his mood. And ever since this early childhood experience, the kite had become a symbol of hope, determination and pure joy for him. Over the years, he had often had reason to have to force his head back up, and it wasn't always easy to search for a kite in the sky – like when his father's ship had got caught in a terrible storm and remains of the vessel were washed ashore for days after; unrequited love; a poor harvest, due to an overlong drought, threatening starvation; and, not so long ago, his mother's departure from this world. But his 'kite philosophy,' even when there was no kite to be found, had never let him down, no matter how hopeless or desperate a situation had seemed. The mere will-power to raise his head up brought with it a newly found strength.

The country had barely recovered from its imbroglio with Portugal and now the war that was raging across the sea, threatened to entangle Spain into the conflict. Today, however, was Pedro's birthday and so he had invited his friends to join him for an outing in the countryside. It was promising to be a glorious, fun-filled day, but the looming war was preying on everybody's mind and dampened the general mood of what should have been a joyous occasion. The young men found it impossible to talk about anything else. The air was heavy with dreams of heroism, fears of separation from loved ones and talks of past horrors of war - the blood, the loss of limbs, the loss of lives.

Even the young ladies, whose interest in the latest court fashion normally took priority over such mundane matters as business and politics, seemed subdued by the gloomy atmosphere without apprehending its full meaning. But how could they grasp a true understanding of war? They might be aware that, for a while, they'd have to forgo acquiring new dresses and would be unable to satisfy their appetites with delicacies; they would suffer from the lack of entertainment, and they would mourn the absence of their friends, fiancés, husbands. But they would never experience the terrors and uncertainties of a battle field. Pedro looked around his group of friends as they sat there with their heads bowed, all sharing the same thoughts – 'How much longer will we be able to enjoy this carefree life? Will we ever be able to meet again like this?'

'My mother used to tell me to always raise my head up high, no matter what, because it encourages resilience and self-esteem,' he told them in an effort to lighten the mood.

'You can't keep looking up when you die,' replied Gonzalez gravely.

'Very true,' they all murmured and nodded in agreement.

Just then, Pedro caught a glimpse of a familiar movement in the distance. He raised his eyes and saw his symbol of hope dance around in the sky. He jumped to his feet shouting, 'Look! Look!' whilst pointing excitedly at the jolly sight above. In an instant everybody had lifted their heads and soon they were all laughing. Then Pedro turned to his friends, 'Isn't it good to raise your head up high? And when you die, where else would you look but to Heaven?'

Entartete Kunst
Degenerate Art, Munich 1937

Degenerate Art

Despite arriving an hour before opening, Maria had to join a seemingly endless queue and endure a long, tedious waiting time before finally being admitted into the building. She walked past the armed guards and followed the signs directing her up a narrow staircase to the first room of the exhibition. She was shocked to find the display in a state of chaos, with the artwork senselessly scattered around the room, and paintings and sculptures jumbled around presenting a scene reminiscent of a flea market. Some oils were hung on thick cord whilst others were just sitting on the floor, propped up against the wall, leaving an overall impression that the exhibition had been curated by a madman. The room was small and soon overcrowded with spectators. Apparently, there were more than 600 works on show, and remembering this made Maria feel nauseous. However, she had come here in search of a particular work by Elfriede Lohse-Wächtler and would not give up before she had found it.

Strassenmusik (Street Music) portrayed a jolly group of men and women parading through the streets with an array of musical instruments, and it was Maria's favourite painting. She used to visit it whenever time permitted. Her mother had first introduced her to the aquarelle, pointing out that one of the musicians bore a strong resemblance to Maria's father, who had died when she was very little. She knew it wasn't really him but there was definitely a strong likeness, especially as her father used to play the trumpet, just like the man depicted in the painting. This beautiful and colourful work had enjoyed a prime position in her local museum and was displayed in its vast atrium near the staircase opposite the entrance. When, two weeks ago, the painting had suddenly disappeared, Maria naturally inquired about its whereabouts. She was told that it had been seized by the *Reichskammer der Bildenden Künste* (Reich Chamber of Visual Art) for their special exhibition entitled 'Degenerate Art'.

Making her way through one crowded room after another, Maria eventually discovered her beloved painting in a room labelled 'Revelation of the Jewish Racial Soul'. The aquarelle, sandwiched between a Kirchner and a Beckmann, hung lop-sided on thick string suspended from a large metal nail. Fitted above was a plaque that read 'An Insult to German Womanhood'. Disregarding the ill-fitting attribution, Maria felt elevated at the sight of it and, like so many times before, immediately lost herself in the merry display.

Maria was still engrossed in her observation when a guard entered the room to announce the arrival of the *Ordnungspolizei* (Order Police) who were to ensure that all was running smoothly for the Reichsminister's visit which was scheduled that very afternoon. A minute later, the police major, flanked by two lieutenants who shoved everybody out of the way, stood, legs apart, in the middle of the room. His green uniform with its shiny buttons seemed brand new. His boots displayed a mirror-like sheen.

The major, disgust written all over his face, marched pompously around between the exhibits. Clutching a copy of the inventory, he appeared to be searching for particular pieces in the collection. As he moved from work to work, the other visitors were expected to make room for him. Maria, too absorbed to notice what was going on around her, had missed her cue for moving along. Incensed by her obliviousness, the major pushed Maria out of the way with his full body weight and sent her flying into one of the paintings which was propped up against the wall. She fell with such force that she went right through the middle of the canvas and hit her head against the stone wall behind it. The oil painting, depicting three female nudes reclining by a pond, was split open and through its large hole Maria could be seen sitting against the wall, but with her legs dangling into the room. 'You imbecile!', bellowed the major.

Maria scrambled to her feet. She looked confused rather than scared.

'Can't you look where you are going, you stupid woman,' he carried on yelling.

'But … ,' stammered Maria, 'you pushed me.'

'What!?' shouted the major, whose face had turned purple. 'You insolent little creature!'

He put his hand on his Luger pistol and with narrowed eyes scanned the surrounding crowd of people. 'Did anybody witness this supposed push?'

'No, no,' everybody murmured as they scattered apart, eager to hurry away to the next room.

The major, not having seen the whole painting, squinted at the damaged remains, observing only the part of canvas still attached to its frame. 'A landscape,' he exclaimed, whilst flicking through his inventory. 'Could have been sold!' he hissed at Maria. 'The Ministry won't be pleased.'

He turned to one of his lieutenants, 'Take this clumsy goose down to headquarters, I shall interrogate her myself. And see to it that nobody moves the damaged painting. I want it left where it is, so the Reichsminister can see why it is necessary to guard this place at all times, despite its despicable contents. Only representatives of the Reich can decide what needs to be destroyed. And ensure the Herr Minister knows that I'm seeing to it personally that the culprit receives appropriate punishment.'

Whilst the major marched around the rest of the exhibition, Maria was escorted to the police headquarters where she was led into a windowless room, furnished with only one table and two chairs. When told to hand over her handbag Maria asked to first retrieve a handkerchief from it. The young lieutenant hesitated for a moment before consenting. But when Maria asked for a glass of water, he shook his head vehemently and declared, 'I'd need the major's permission for that, and he won't be back for a while.'

So Maria waited patiently, nodding off a couple of times, until finally she heard the door being unlocked, and the major entered. He flung himself noisily into the chair opposite Maria and stared at her in silence. A minute later, the young officer appeared, carrying a steaming cup of coffee which he set down in front of his superior.

'Can I have some water, please,' asked Maria again.

The major gave her a cynical smile. 'Sure,' he said coldly, 'once we have established some facts.'

He slurped noisily at his coffee before opening a large folder. 'Name,' he said without looking up.

'Maria Dressler.'

'Would you say, Fräulein Dressler, that you are generally a clumsy person?'

'No, not at all,' replied Maria incensed at the assumption.

'Alright then, what else made you stagger into that painting?'

'You did!' she replied sternly. 'And I didn't stagger, I fell … because *you* pushed me.'

The major shook his head. 'This attitude of yours is not getting us anywhere,' he said gravely. 'And it certainly won't get you any water!' he suddenly shouted. Then, adapting a calm tone again, he continued. 'Now, am I correct, and it's in your best interest not to contradict me, that you were deliberately destroying one of the few works, amongst the otherwise detestable exhibits, that could have been sold? With the sole intent of preventing the German Reich from gaining financially?'

'Definitely not! I strongly object to these allegations.'

He looked at her wide-eyed and with raised eyebrows. 'You object, do you?', he said slowly.

'Strongly,' declared Maria. 'You see, I love art, and I think these paintings are wonderful,' she said passionately. 'I would never do anything to damage them.'

'I see!,' exclaimed the major delightedly. 'This is worse than I thought. You consider these abhorrent presentations, these mockeries of the Deutsche Kunst and all that our Heimatland stands for, to be wonderful?! You are a traitor!'

Most excited at this new development, he leaned back in his chair, the fingers of his left hand tapping furiously on the table.

'No, I just meant ...'

But the major would not let her finish. 'Quiet now,' he snapped. 'No more arguments!'

After a brief moment, he leaned forward and smiled sweetly at Maria before addressing her in a mellifluous voice. 'Mein liebes Fraulein, you have three options, and I shall help you make the right decision because you are young and attractive, I don't want to see your life cut short. I'm a Mensch, after all. But, I can only do so much.'

'What options,' asked Maria suspiciously.

'You are either a traitor, a saboteur or a clumsy, disturbed individual.'

'But none of it is true.'

'That's not for you to decide, my dear. What you need to do is choose which one you want to be punished for. As a traitor, you'll be sentenced to death, but it'll be quick – all over in a few minutes. The current procedure for disturbed individuals is an indefinite stay in a sanatorium for observation and medical trials. As a saboteur, you'll be looking at a prison term of … well, with a recommendation from me, a few months maximum. I think we'll opt for sabotage, shall we?'

Maria, shocked and frightened, just nodded.

'So,' he smiled at her, 'let's wrap this up, shall we.' He handed her a pre-printed confession form and a pen and dictated,

'I, Maria Dressler, plead guilty to having deliberately destroyed a painting in an act of sabotage against the German Reich.'

'Now, sign here,' he snapped, pointing at the dotted line further down the page.

The major snatched the sheet of paper from her. 'See, all done. And you can have a nice glass of water now.' He got up and shouted for the guard.

'Saboteur, as I thought,' he told the young lieutenant. Then added quietly, 'Take her to block C, no visitors for the first five months.'

Back at his desk, the major poured himself a large brandy in celebration of yet another successful day. Proud of his achievement, he then reclined in his chair and scoured the room with a self-satisfied smile.

Maria and her gaoler had hardly disappeared out of sight when a courier arrived with an urgent message from the *Reichsministerium für Volksaufklärung und Propaganda* (Ministry of Public Enlightenment and Propaganda). Convinced that it would be a note of praise because the Reichsminister had been impressed with his efficiency in dealing with this case of sabotaged vandalism, Polizeimajor Hofer, full of pride, tore open the envelope.

"*Demand immediate release of Fräulein Maria Dressler who, by destroying a scandalous pornographic painting, is to be decorated with the highest honour for her services to German Art!*"

Signed,

Joseph Goebbels

(RMVP – Reichsministerium für Volksaufklärung und Propaganda)

'Oh,' uttered the major stunned. A second later he turned to the messenger, 'It is *I* who deserve the award. After all, *I* pushed her!'

Gustav Klimt
Two Girls With Oleander (Zwei Mädchen mit Oleander), 1890-92

Two Girls With Oleander

'Meet me at two,' shouted Frederike across the hall to Anna, who was on her way to the music room for her weekly piano lesson. There was no need to mention where. Ever since they were little girls they would tell each other stories, exchange secrets and complaints, all in the same meeting place – the oleander tree at the bottom of the winter garden. A plant as beautiful as it was deadly! When they were very young, the girls were constantly warned not to touch any part of the tree as it was highly poisonous in its entirety. It was but a little shrub when it was first planted but, like Frederike and Anna, it grew tall, and blossomed more and more with maturity.

Anna had been adopted by Frederike's parents when she was three, after her own parents died in a yachting accident in the Mediterranean Sea. Luckily, Anna had stayed behind with her nurse that day. Anna's and Frederike's parents had been friends since childhood, and the moment Herr and Frau Weinberg heard of their friends' tragic end, they decided to provide a home for the little orphan. Frederike was five at the time and immediately threw herself into the role of older sister. Anna had been welcomed into the Weinberg family with such enthusiasm that she soon felt at home at the magnificent Palais located in Vienna's finest district. She was therefore utterly surprised when she was told shortly after her sixteenth birthday that Mr and Mrs Weinberg were not her biological parents. The timing of the decision to inform Anna about her real identity was influenced by the young lady having attracted an admirer who, so smitten by Anna's beauty, had asked for her hand in marriage. Mr and Mrs Weinberg were delighted about Graf Liebenstein's proposal. The Graf was very wealthy and of excellent social standing, which meant that Anna's future was secured. As for the Weinbergs, Graf Liebenstein couldn't have chosen a better moment to take Anna off their hands. Mr Weinberg's business had not been flourishing lately so for Anna to become somebody else's responsibility would ease his financial burden substantially.

At the time of Anna's parents' death, Mr Weinberg was one of the wealthiest and most influential people in Vienna. So he readily accepted the condition set by Herr Hofner, Anna's uncle, for the adoption of his niece, which meant that Anna would only receive a modest sum of her parents' fortune, whilst Herr Hofner would inherit the rest. Ludwig Hofner was a despicable man and he had a wife to match. Anna's parents always said that they hoped the pair would never have children as they would pity any child having to live with such mean spirited people. Herr and Frau Weinberg cared deeply about little Anna and did not hesitate to agree to her uncle's unfair terms. Anna's wellbeing was all that mattered.

Anna found herself in emotional turmoil – the news about her parentage, followed immediately by a marriage proposal left her in a state of confusion. Of course, she was flattered by the proposal, especially as Frederike, who was two years older than her, hadn't had one yet. On the other hand, Anna didn't feel ready to be married. She was free spirited and eager for knowledge, she did not want to put her own needs and interests aside and she had no intention of arranging her life to fit in with a man's wishes, no matter how wealthy or handsome he might be. Anna didn't know if Graf Liebenstein was handsome, she had never met him. Apparently, he had noticed her first at the opera where she and Frederike were regular attendees. It was her passionate and open display of emotions during a performance of Rigoletto when she had first caught his eye. That he was wealthy, she'd assumed as his name was often mentioned in the best circles of Viennese society. But had she had any doubts regarding his financial status, Herr Weinberg cleared that up when he first told Anna of the proposal. Having received Herr Weinberg's blessing, Graf Liebenstein was due to call on Anna the very next day to propose to her directly. Anna couldn't wait to talk to Frederike.

It was the longest piano lesson Anna had ever had to endure. Even when her teacher, who'd realised that she wasn't her usual self, suggested that she should play a Gavotte, which Anna loved and always played with such ease and enthusiasm, she found it impossible to concentrate and was unable to give a musically worthy rendition. When she finally arrived at the oleander tree, Frederike was already waiting. 'You poor thing,' exclaimed Frederike, flinging her arms round her rather perplexed sister.

'Why,' asked Anna, 'because I'm not your real sister or because I'm getting married?'

'Both! But mainly because of the proposal, or rather because of the suitor. You mustn't accept.'

'Do you know Graf Liebenstein?'

'Mama pointed him out once … at the opera when you were ill and she was accompanying me instead. He is old, Anna! He is … oh … fifty years old! And he wants a pretty young wife to bear him a child!'

'Our father, if I can still call him that, seemed very excited about the idea.'

'Oh, Anna,' exclaimed Frederike hugging her sister again, 'of course you can continue to call him what you have called him for the past thirteen years! In the same way that I am your sister, no matter what! And whilst Papa may like the idea of you marrying Liebenstein, he would never force you into it!'

Frederike's reaction scared Anna and got her very worried. What if the Graf was really old and ugly? What if she hated him? It is all very well for her sister to say she shouldn't accept the Graf, but she wasn't present when their father made the announcement. He was so full of joy and ebullience, and gave no indication that she had a choice. In fact, he mentioned how relieved he was in view of the family's current financial dilemma. Anna felt burdened to do her duty regardless, whether she liked the Graf or not. The Weinberg's had taken her in, given her a home, brought her up like their own daughter. She could not repay them with disobedience. She wondered though if Frederike, had she been the recipient of the proposal, would have been expected to oblige her father's wishes. 'Frederike,' Anna whispered, 'I shall meet the Graf tomorrow and then make the right decision.'

'Good,' replied Frederike, 'as long as you follow your heart.'

Whatever Anna's expectations, Graf Liebenstein exceeded them. His white beard speckled here and there with grey; the remnants of hair mainly concentrated at either side rather than on the top of his head; the protruding stomach and the stooping bulk of his overweight body leaning heavily on a sturdy walking stick, all contributed to the overall impression of a man far beyond fifty years of age. He was, in fact, near seventy. If Anna had a shock when she first laid eyes on him, her exceptional good manners concealed any disappointment or negativity she might have felt towards him.

Graf Liebenstein was an economical conversationalist. He presented his proposal as a business rather than a romantic proposition wherein his future wife would be amply compensated for her labours. Anna could do whatever she desired, providing she bore him at least one child, more should time permit him. In return, she could spend as much money as she liked during his lifetime as well as becoming the sole heir of his extensive fortune. He also pledged to settle Mr Weinberg's creditors. Anna listened attentively and respectfully and promised him an answer by the end of the week.

Herr and Frau Weinberg, whilst insisting that they only had Anna's best interest for a secure future in mind, urged their adopted daughter to accept the Graf's generous offer, even hinting at the Graf's failing health. So however repulsed Anna must have felt at the prospect of sharing the old man's bed, she still accepted his proposal. Frederike was devastated. She begged Anna to reconsider, pleaded with her parents to intercept, but all to no avail. The Weinberg's saw Anna's marriage as the only way out of their financial dire straits, and Anna had convinced herself that it was her duty to come to their rescue.

Shortly after the wedding, the Graf insisted they retreat to his castle in Liebenstein, where they remained until the autumn. During her time away, Anna abstained from all social activity unless her attendance was a specific request from her husband. And although she corresponded frequently with Frederike and her parents, she never invited them to visit. Not that she didn't want to see them, rather she missed them too much and she feared she wouldn't be able to endure another separation. Losing them so abruptly after the wedding, had already been more than she could bear.

Still, she had done her duty. Conception was an ordeal, but at least she got impregnated very quickly and, once confirmed, she was excused from that duty until after the birth. By the time she returned to Vienna, Anna was six months pregnant. The first thing Anna did after arriving in her palatial Viennese residence was to write a note to Frederike: 'Meet me tomorrow at three.'

The moment Anna set foot in her childhood home, she had to fight back the tears. Did they know how much she'd sacrificed? How she hated being separated from them? How little she cared about her husband's wealth? How she loathed his lecherous looks, his vile touch? She hurried towards the oleander tree where Frederike already waited with outstretched arms.

'I have missed you so much,' whispered Frederike in Anna's ear whilst letting her tears flow unashamedly. Anna just clung to her sister, so overcome by emotions that she was unable to talk. Frederike explained that their parents had spent a few days in the country and were not expected back until the evening, but were so looking forward to seeing her. 'So you must stay for dinner, or better still, spend the night if you can,' she pleaded. 'But in the meantime, we have the whole afternoon to ourselves!'

Frederike stepped back and held Anna at arms' length, 'You look radiant,' she smiled at her pregnant sister, admiring her blushed cheeks, her glowing skin, her overall perfect complexion, whilst not failing to notice that Anna's eyes had lost their sparkle, their liveliness, and instead Frederike detected in them a deep sadness that bordered on bitterness. 'How is it,' Frederike forced herself to sound cheerful. 'Tell me everything!'

'I don't think I should tell you everything,' stated Anna with grievous seriousness. 'It would put you off marriage and that wouldn't be fair, because I'm sure there are cases where it is a wonderful experience. And I sincerely wish that for you.'

Frederike gasped in horror and started crying again. 'Oh, Anna,' she wailed, 'I told you not to marry him, I advised you to refuse him. Why did you go ahead with it?'

'It was our parents' wish, and they were always so good to me, how could I …'

'Wish, maybe, but they would not have forced you! Nobody would have seriously expected you to make such a sacrifice.'

It was Anna's turn now to lose control of her composure. She threw herself into her sister's arms and sobbed uncontrollably, as if she was hoping to wash away the ordeal of the last few months with her tears. 'The first few weeks were the worst,' she sobbed. 'He demanded to lie with me whenever he felt his body was able to function properly to produce an heir, whether day or night. And even when his manhood failed him, he would still insist on groping at all my intimate body parts. Often, he made me expose myself to him in bright daylight when he would drool over my naked body whilst making vulgar noises.'

'My poor, poor darling,' shrieked Frederike, devastated by her sister's account. 'I thought he would at least be a gentleman!'

'Once I was with child,' continued Anna trying to stop her tears, 'it got better. He would still insist on touching me inappropriately whenever he felt like it, but he would refrain from trying to enter me.' Overcome by the mere thought of it, Anna suddenly screamed, 'I don't think I can bear it any longer!'

Frederike could think of no words of comfort that could possibly ease her sister's destiny so she just held her in her arms and stroked her gently. Whilst waiting for Anna to calm down, an idea started to form in Frederike's head. Once Anna had regained some composure, Frederike guided her closer to the oleander tree. Smiling faintly, she picked a few blossoms off the tree and whispered, 'Some of these mixed in with his supper, and all your problems will be solved.'

Shart
Young Girl With A Lamp
(Jeune Fille A La Lampe), 1968
© Shart Estate

Young Girl With A Lamp

She jumped up as soon as she heard the knock, shocked that she had allowed herself to fall asleep. She didn't know what time it was, nor did she care. He was here, that was all that mattered. She grabbed the dimly lit lamp and hurried to the door. Her heart was pounding as it always did just thinking of him, and had done since their first encounter.

He was the most handsome man she had ever laid eyes on. 'A stranger,' they said, 'only arrived in the village that morning.' He had stopped at her stall and looked at the various shells on offer but she could sense that he was not interested in any of them. He picked up a small tiger shell and let his finger glide across the opening whilst, unashamedly, fixing his dark, fiery eyes on her. She did not dare meet his gaze, but she could feel him looking her over, and it took her breath away. Nobody had ever exposed her like this … with a mere glance.

'I see you've met my wife,' came Nathan's booming voice from behind her, making her raise her eyes as if by reflex and finding herself staring at the stranger opposite.

'I guess I have,' replied the newcomer without averting his gaze from her.

'Margaret, this is John Matheson, a new hand I hired during my last trip,' Nathan explained whilst walking past her towards John. He put his hand on John's shoulder, 'Come, I'll show you round the shipyard.'
Margaret was determined to avoid the stranger but, despite being aware of the danger of seeing him again, she could not stay away. She was drawn to him by a force that she had never before experienced. What she felt for him was so alien to her that she was unable to interpret its meaning. His presence scared her; his absence she found unbearable. Every day she thought of another reason to venture down to the harbour

to visit her husband's shipyard - to check on the catch of the day because she wanted a particular fish for supper; to stock up on unusual shells; or to bring something to her husband which she was sure he needed but had forgotten to take himself. And every time, John would hang around just where she'd pretend she needed to be. Their encounters were brief but John appeared more daring with every meeting. It had started with an exchange of a few words, always prompted by him. Once, when taking a basket of fruit from her, he had placed his hands on top of hers and his fingers stroked her wrists before he allowed her to withdraw them from his grasp. That night, when her husband had demanded his marital right, she'd kept her eyes tightly shut and thought of John.

A few days later, when she was again looking for Nathan to bring him a scarf, which she believed he should be wearing now that it was getting colder, one of the workmen sent her to one of the warehouses. 'You just missed Nathan', came John's soft tenor from the darkness. And, before her eyes had even adjusted to the unlit surroundings, she suddenly felt his strong arm around her waist, pulling her tenderly but firmly towards him. She didn't struggle, she just let it happen. A kiss so full of longing and passion, she could feel her legs giving way. Had he not held her so tightly, she would have slumped to the floor. She was still dizzy and disorientated when he released her. 'Nathan,' he whispered, 'will leave tomorrow for a couple of days. He won't need me to come along. I'll be with you tomorrow night.'

Nathan was a good man but, had Margaret had a say in it, she would not have chosen him for her life companion. When her father died, Margaret's mother was grateful that Nathan offered to marry her fourteen year old daughter, with the promise to also look after the mother. Nathan kept his word. He not only supported the old woman financially until her death, he also allowed Margaret to tend to her during illness. And, despite the age difference between them, he always treated his young wife with the utmost respect. In return, Margaret had always fulfilled her part in every aspect of her wifely duties. She did not want to intentionally hurt her husband but nor did she feel guilty in succumbing to a sensation that had so far been beyond her reach, beyond even her wildest imagination. Nathan no more deserved to be betrayed, than she did to live without ever experiencing love and passion. She did not think of the consequences her adventure might have, did not wonder what the next day might bring. Caution, reason, her future – all seemed irrelevant compared to the excitement and exhilaration she felt.

Her naked body barely covered by the skimpy dressing gown, she rushed to the door, oblivious to the storm that raged outside, thinking only of John and of throwing herself into his arms. Impatiently she forced back the bolts and flung open the door.

'You shouldn't open the door so willingly', scolded Nathan. 'Especially when you are here on your own. It could have been a stranger knocking.'

Margaret staggered back, shocked, worried, disappointed, wondering whether John was aware that her husband's travel had been sabotaged by the weather. And what if they had missed their only opportunity of being together? Aware suddenly of the chill in the air and her flimsy, inappropriate attire she walked over to the window to retrieve the thick woollen blanket off the armchair. As she wrapped herself into it, she saw a tall shadow of a figure battling against the storm, making his way towards the harbour, away from the house, away from her. An overwhelming sense of loss made it impossible to force back the tears as she watched her little glimpse of happiness, for which she was prepared to risk everything, slip away. Something in his stride – the forcefulness, the determination to disappear - told her that he would not return.

Frans Hals
The Gypsy Girl, 1628

The Gypsy Girl

She gave him a coquettish smile whilst shaking her ample and immodestly exposed bosom from side to side. 'Please, sir, take a seat,' she chirped. 'Only one guilder for both - to read your palm and consult the cards to see what happiness your future will bring.' With a dismissive gesture he offered her the money. She took the coin and put it in a small leather pouch that dangled from her left hip. Sitting down opposite him she reached across the little table and took his hand. Calmly she scanned over his palm for a few seconds before raising her big dark eyes in horror and alarm to meet his cynical grin.

'What,' he asked bemused, 'short lifeline?'

She didn't answer. Her only response was to let go off his hand and shrink back in her seat as if he were poisonous. Then her expression softened into a sad, pitying look.

'Come on,' he coaxed, 'tell me! I can take it.'

She got up and, turning away from him, whispered, 'I'm sorry, Sir. You have to leave.'

'No way,' he exclaimed cheerfully, 'we're going to do the cards next. You are not cheating me out of that, I've paid for the whole hocus pocus, so let's have it.'

He did not believe in fortune telling and always referred to the entire profession as a bunch of charlatans and thieves but, after a day out drinking with his friends, he told his companions that he was going to do it for a laugh, betting that he'd be promised a long and happy life, probably even romance. The young gypsy girl, having stepped out of her tent earlier to soak up some of the sweet summer air, had overheard his mocking and decided to teach him a lesson. She would usually make a genuine effort to please people but some customers, like this one, did not deserve to be treated kindly.

Not put off by his initial carefree reaction, she took the pack of cards and again settled down across from him. She had done this so many times that, even without the secret markings, she would have had no problem in finding the appropriate card. She turned over death, gasping with horror at the apparently unexpected sight of it. The black reaper is not necessarily a bad omen, but most people are alarmed by the image of him. She was sure it would do the trick with this arrogant young man. On top of that, her performance was skilfully dramatic.

'What does it mean,' he asked.

'Please go now,' she pleaded.

She even thought of offering him his money back for added effect but then decided against it. He was still grinning but there was something unsettling in his voice when he asked, 'What is it? What do you think you've seen?'

'I don't like telling people bad things,' she gasped. 'I really don't want to upset anybody. I am a fortune-teller, not a bearer of bad news. And anyway, even if you knew, you cannot change your destiny. So please go and enjoy the rest of your life.' Then, giving him her most pitiful look, she added very quietly but definitely audibly, 'The rest of this night.'

'You can't seriously believe this nonsense,' he muttered whilst staggering outside to re-join his friends. 'Just as I predicted,' he laughed, 'love, happiness and fortune shall all be mine before long!'

'That was not very nice of you,' came a voice from behind a curtain.

'He got what he deserved, mother,' the girl replied dismissively.

The older woman drew back the curtain, 'Maybe, but your jape just proved his point.'

'Even if I had taken it seriously, he would not. You should have heard him, how he mocked us. He was mean and disrespectful of what we do.'

'So were you just now. And in any case, it doesn't matter if he believes what you tell him or not – he paid you to do what you had offered, even if he thinks we are all charlatans. ... And cover yourself up, put a shawl round your shoulders. People will get the wrong idea about what you're offering.'

The young girl just shrugged her shoulders, 'I don't care what people think. Men though seem to like the way I look, and I like them looking at me.'

Then, defiance written all over her face, she adjusted her blouse in a way that threatened to reveal even more flesh before walking outside to see whether she could attract new customers. Despite it being a Saturday night, business was slow. By ten o'clock, she had had enough and wanted to go home but her mother insisted she persevered for another couple of hours, reminding her daughter that often a very quiet evening could suddenly get busy just before midnight. It was a warm summer's night, but the air felt heavy and thick. The young girl picked up a wooden stool and sat down right outside the entrance to their brightly coloured tent. When she saw the dark figure turning the corner, she immediately jumped up and started her chant, 'Good fortune for you, good sir. Only one guilder to read your palm but I can also ...' Smiling, he suddenly lunged at her, grabbed her by the hair and pulled her head back to place a large knife at her throat. She hadn't recognised him until he hissed in her ear,

'What awful, unspeakable thing is going to happen to me? What did you see?'

'Nothing,' she quivered, 'please, it was a mistake.'

'Don't lie! … There's no point, because whatever happens to me tonight, will also happen to you. So we shall soon see what horrible destiny lies ahead.'

He moved the knife from her throat to her side whilst putting his other arm around her waist and grabbing her tightly, thus forcing her to accompany him. Faint flashes of light in the distance followed by a succession of quietly rumbling thunder promised relief from the stifling heat.

'Where are we going,' she panted as he hurried her along the cobbled street, but he did not answer. Instead, he manoeuvred her onto a small path to the right that led straight towards the nearby forest. She wasn't particularly frightened at first. After all, she had invented his destiny. Then again, fear can drive people to madness, or to do all sorts of horrible things. As she quietly argued this, she came to the conclusion that it was best to tell him the truth. Having succeeded with her initial intention of scaring him, she couldn't help smiling at her achievement whilst starting to confess.

'I made it all up,' she burst out. 'I'm so sorry, but I heard how irreverently you spoke about our people, our profession to your friends and thought that I'd teach you a lesson.'

Words came tumbling out and she didn't seem to catch a breath until she had revealed everything. Only then did she realise that they had stopped walking and he was now facing her, laughing heartily. She saw that the knife, illuminated by another streak of lightning, although still firm in his hand, was not pressed against her anymore but resting against the side of his leg. Relieved by his good humour, she too started giggling. And the roaring roll of thunder seemed to join in.

When, a few seconds later, he went up in flames, she instinctively started to run away as fast as she could. The bolt of lightning had struck so furiously and so fast that the moment she had seen it, it had set him alight.

Vincent Van Gogh
Two Peasant Women Digging Potatoes, 1885

Two Peasant Women Digging Potatoes

'Almost done,' exhaled Birgit breathlessly in an attempt to encourage Gudrun who seemed even more exhausted than she. 'These should last us all winter.' It was an unusually cold start to the autumn, and maybe they should have harvested a couple of weeks earlier. They will know better next year.

'Yes,' replied Gudrun whilst trying to find the strength to push the shovel once more into the hard ground. 'And let it not be said that no good can ever come of evil.'

The two women had been digging for hours. Their hands, sore from blisters that had burst and reformed numerous times, were sticking to the wooden handles of their tools. Their backs, by now comfortable in their hunched over position, had stopped aching - as long as they didn't try to stand upright. It was their first potato crop, but not the first time they had dug up the same plot of land. And by comparison, this time was nowhere near as laborious as when they had to dig deep enough to bury their father. They didn't mind hard work or a few aches and pains. Nor did they mind working the field in the bitter cold. It was a small price to pay for a quiet life.

Birgit was the older of the Huisen sisters. She was five years old when Gudrun was born. So when, a few years later, their mother died, it fell to Birgit to look after Gudrun, which she did as best she could, in addition to keeping the house clean, feeding the animals, doing the cooking, and tending to their father. From an early age, Gudrun had to help her sister with some of the simpler tasks. It wasn't an easy life but it was the only one they knew, and the girls did what was expected of them without complaining. What else could they have done? They had to take over their mother's role. It was only a small holding, but sufficient enough to keep them from starving. They had a few sheep, some chickens, one cow and two old horses. Once every few weeks, Mr Huisen would load up the wagon with whatever produce he could scrape together and set off on the two day journey to the nearest village to try and sell his goods, or exchange them for anything they didn't grow or couldn't make themselves. Birgit and Gudrun had never been to the village. Their father wouldn't allow it because, apparently, it was a dangerous place for children and women, and in any case, they couldn't desert the farm.

When Birgit, aged 13, gave birth to her first child, Gudrun was terrified at the sound of her sister's screams. All night it went on until late morning when Birgit's cries were finally replaced by those of her baby girl. The sisters were delighted and thought she was the most beautiful thing they ever saw, more so than the little chicks or the spring lambs, or even the baby rabbits with their fluffy fur and floppy ears which had always been their favourites because they were able to stroke them and pick them up. She was such a sweet little thing, with big blue eyes, plump red cheeks and a tiny tuft of blond hair. But Mr. Huisen insisted the baby had a dangerous disease, and unless he got rid of it, it would infect all of them and they would all die. No matter how much Birgit and Gudrun objected and argued, Mr Huisen would not even let Birgit feed the baby before he took her away. Birgit bore several more children, as did Gudrun – all suffering, according to Mr Huisen, from the same fatal, highly contagious illness - until last year, when Gudrun finally gave birth to a healthy boy. Sadly, Gudrun had suffered more then during any other delivery and developed a very high fever. Birgit nursed her sister day and night but the fever would not break. She begged her father to get a doctor from the village but he replied that no doctor could help Gudrun. It was good though that Birgit, having recently given birth herself to another diseased girl, was able to nurse the little boy. She gently picked him up and put her nipple into his screaming mouth, just as she had seen her mother do after Gudrun was born. Within seconds the little mouth started sucking greedily until, satisfied and exhausted, he fell asleep in her arms. Birgit couldn't stop her tears as she watched the tiny little creature sleeping so peacefully. How much she would have loved to nurse at least one of her babies, how she longed for one of her girls to be alive.

One night, Birgit was woken by some muffled sounds coming from Gudrun's bed. As she looked up, she saw her father standing over Gudrun pressing a thick blanket over her face. Birgit jumped up and screamed at him to stop, but he wouldn't listen. She tried to pull him away, but he pushed her aside mumbling, 'Too many mouths to feed … she'll die anyway, better to speed things up.'

In desperation, Birgit grabbed hold of the iron poker in the corner. She started to hit her father but he would not let go of the blanket. So she continued to hit him until his head was a bloody mess and his body fell motionless to the floor. She hurried to her sister's side. Gudrun was fitful and breathing heavily, but she was alive. Birgit dragged the dead body outside into the freezing cold and left it next to the barn. She would think of a way to dispose of it later, right now Gudrun and the baby were her priority. Birgit had no regrets about what she had done. She'd despised her father ever since he took her first baby away. And she'd hated having to lay down again and again to give him another chance to create more babies to kill.

Within a few days, Gudrun made a full recovery. She had some recollection of somebody trying to suffocate her, but assumed she had been hallucinating due to her high fever. Once aware of what had taken place, she was grateful to Birgit because Gudrun too had come to loath their cruel father. The sisters had suspected for some time that there was nothing wrong with any of the girls they had borne and that their father's only reason for killing them was because he did not want to hand out any more food, unless the baby was a boy. The sisters were confident that they could look after themselves and little Hannes as they decided to call Gudrun's little boy. And they were hoping to bear more baby girls in future, the moment Hannes was old enough to father them.

Anonymous
The Photograph, C. 1915

The Photograph

When Jack returned from his annual visit to his paternal grandparents he found his father waiting for him at the station. Jack loved his father and was pleased to see him, but he absolutely adored his mother and had missed her dreadfully these last three weeks. Naturally, he assumed that she had missed him too, so he was disappointed that she hadn't accompanied his father to collect him. When asked where she was, his father said he'd explain once they got home.

Apparently his mother had been ill for some time, although her death was rather sudden. They thought it best not to tell Jack whilst he was away, and decided to get the funeral out of the way before his return, as it would be far too upsetting for a seven year old child to attend such a sombre and sad event. That night, and many subsequent ones, Jack cried himself to sleep. If only he could have seen her one more time. He still had so much to tell her. If only he could have said goodbye. All he had left of her was an old photograph, taken a few years before he was born. She looked so happy and beautiful and kind in it – just as he remembered her. The photograph became his most treasured possession. It would never leave his side – at night, he'd place it on his bedside table, during the day he'd carry it around in his pocket. With this photograph he could keep his mother's memory alive. It was a way of sharing his happy times and his sorrow with her, and without it he would probably have forgotten over the years what she looked like. He was so grateful for the existence of that photograph, he'd later decided to become a photographer himself, because he wanted to create memories for other people.

He had such passion for the craft that he excelled in it. His attention to detail in capturing the realistic essence of people bordered almost on obsession. He placed all emphasis on the memory aspect of his creation and insisted that the final image of his sitter had to be a true depiction of how the person wanted to be remembered. In most cases, he encouraged his subjects to aim for an expression that would best replicate the happiest day in their lives. As his reputation grew, his business thrived. He was soon able to open a studio where he worked relentlessly to produce happy memories for strangers that would one day become heirlooms.

He was so much in demand that people had to make appointments to have their photograph taken by him. So when one day a lady walked in off the street and asked very shyly if he would be able to fit her in, he at first turned her away. She said she understood that he was very busy but pleaded that she would only be in town that day and that this was her only chance of having a memory of herself created for someone she loved. This touched him so deeply that he agreed to postpone his next appointment in favour of her. She was not a young woman but she was attractive and he thought she must have been very beautiful once. He was determined to make this lost beauty reappear. Her eyes were sad, and he knew, in order to recapture some past happiness, he had to make her smile through them. He set up his camera ready to take her back to happier times. As he adjusted the focus, he suddenly saw through his lens what he hadn't detected with the naked eye. Slowly he stepped back, took out his most precious possession, and held out the photograph. He stared at the woman as her ashen face started to glisten from the stream of meaningless tears. 'Why?' he asked.

'I fell in love,' she whispered, 'and I was young.'

'I was younger still, and I needed you. You were my universe. Why could you not love me when I loved you so much?'

'I wanted to contact you but your father …'

'My father,' he interrupted her, 'was protecting me! He must have thought it was kinder to let me believe that you were dead rather than telling me you had abandoned me … and I thank him for that.'

He tore up the photograph in front of her. 'Photographs,' he said as he showed her out of the door, 'create false memories.'

He locked up his studio never to set foot in it again.

Édouard Manet
Boating, 1874

Boating

'Oh, Pierre,' she sighed, 'what a lovely idea to spend the afternoon lazing around on a boat. And such a perfect way to take advantage of the first proper summer day!'

Despite not being able to swim, Celine loved the water. She would often stroll down to the lake and, during warm summer days, sit for hours on the gently sloping bank, sometimes to read or paint, other times to just breathe in the calmness of the water. But she would only venture out in a boat if accompanied by a very competent swimmer.

'And it's good to be alone and sheltered from prying eyes,' Pierre replied in a sombre, joyless manner. His unromantic tone upset her. It reminded her of the dreary reality of her situation – she was his lover, his mistress, not his wife - that's why they could not be seen together in public. In the beginning, Celine found the secrecy added to the excitement of their relationship, just as the uncertainty of each meeting increased their longing for each other. After a few months though, she got tired of playing hide and seek. But Pierre had always made it quite clear that he could never leave his wife, although he was adamant that he did not love her. Celine, however, was confident that she would be able to change his mind, in light of the new development.

'I swear I could feel a tiny kick the other day,' ventured Celine whilst putting her hand on her tummy.

'Impossible,' replied Pierre without a hint of compassion, 'the thing isn't properly formed yet, it certainly won't have any limbs'. He hesitated before continuing, 'That's why it would still be easy to get rid of it. This old nurse I know would …'

'No,' she snapped back, 'I told you, there'll be no abortion! I really want this child, your child. And I know you will adore this little baby,' she added sweetly. 'Soon, I'll be showing though, so I think it's time to tell your wife. I know she'll be very upset, but even if she doesn't set you free, she ought to know at least, and maybe, in time, after the baby is born, she will let us live together in peace.'

Pierre loved Celine, more than any of his past mistresses, but leaving his wife was out of the question, and he had no intention of ever admitting to adultery. He could not survive without his wife's family fortune – he would lose his social standing, his luxurious life style and all the privilege associated with it. He was not going to jeopardise his existence.

'Celine,' he addressed her gently, deciding to attempt once more to make her see sense, 'we cannot have this child together, you do realise that? Nobody must ever know that I'm the father.'

'You said you loved me, swore that you were never in love with her and yet …'

'That's right, but love has nothing to do with it. That's what makes it all so complicated. If love was the deciding factor, all would be so simple.'

'So your choice is based on money? You are choosing your wife's wealth over me? Over love? Over happiness?'

'No, you are! Because you are forcing me to make this choice. I'd rather choose a way that can afford me all – you, love, happiness, and wealth – simply by staying married and keeping our relationship just between the two of us.'

This blatant admission, the fact that he wasn't even trying to hide his philandering intention made her absolutely furious. 'You bastard,' she hissed. 'And what would I get out of this whilst you have everything?'

'You knew I was married,' he continued calmly, 'when you first agreed to let me kiss you in Fernand's tiny study whilst my wife was sitting downstairs playing cards. And you knew my circumstances when you agreed to meet me at the hotel d'Abre a week later.'

'Yes, and I was prepared to have an affair … I didn't expect to fall in love with you, but I did … and you with me, I know it. And that changed things.'

'Nothing has changed,' Pierre replied angrily. 'I never promised you anything. I love you too, Celine, I really do. But if you insist on having this child, you are on your own. You will never see me again. Is that clear?'

Celine, in her anger and frustration at realising the hopelessness of her situation, rather than trying to appease Pierre, reacted in a way that ggravated him even more and sent him into an uncontainable panic.

'You are not going to wriggle out of this,' she shouted. 'This child,' she pointed wildly at her abdomen, 'is your responsibility. And I shall make sure to tell anybody who is prepared to listen!'

If Pierre had been irresolute about how to prevent his wife from finding out about his infidelity and how to stop his young, pregnant lover ruining his future, then Celine had just helped him reach a decision. If only she hadn't threatened him because until then, he had hoped to find an amicable solution. Even this morning he had prayed to god that Celine would understand his predicament. And when he saw her running towards the boat, so happy, carefree, uncomplicated, he was almost convinced that all would end well, and it wouldn't have to come to this. But how could he ignore a threat like that? He would never be able to trust her to keep their secret; he would spend every minute of every day in fear of discovery. His wife might forgive him another affair, but she would never forgive him fathering another woman's child when she herself had been unable to conceive.

To emphasise how serious she was about exposing him, Celine was leaning towards Pierre and had raised a finger menacingly when Pierre suddenly jumped up and bounced at the side of the boat with such force that it capsized. Celine was so surprised by the precipitous movement that she barely made a sound. Only, once in the water, did she whimper and cry whilst flapping her arms hysterically. Pierre swam towards her and she must have thought that he was coming to her rescue, but instead he pushed her head under the water and guided her body underneath the turned-over boat. It didn't take long before her body became motionless. To make sure though, he continued to swim around the boat in a frantic manner. Had there been any on-lookers on the shore, they would have verified that he was searching for something. After he considered enough time to have lapsed, he swam to the shore, shouting 'Help! Help! A girl! She's drowning!'

Juan Gris
Still Life With Checked Tablecloth, 1915

Still Life With Checked Tablecloth

'Where are you going, Mary?' asked Tom Warren as he watched his wife picking up the car keys.

'To the shops,' she replied. 'We have no lemons left.'

'I'll drive you,' he volunteered.

'There's no need,' she'd protested, but he had already snatched the keys out of her hand.

As he turned into the main road and stopped at the traffic lights, which had just changed to yellow, a motorbike zoomed passed them and crossed the junction by red.

'Did you see that?!' he hissed.

'No,' she replied uninterestedly, 'I wasn't really paying attention.'

'Good thing I'm driving then,' he grunted.

'You stay where you are!' he snarled at the car trying to etch into his lane from the right. 'If you think I'll let you cut in, think again!' He quickly accelerated, almost bumping into the car in front of him whilst giving the driver of the Mercedes coming out of the side road on his left a threatening look.

'They can't hear you,' she needlessly pointed out. 'I don't know why you insist on talking to the other cars.'

'Something wrong with your indicator,' he shouted at the Volvo in front which turned right at the junction without indicating. 'And where the hell does he think he's going,' he complained as he cut off a cyclist who tried to overtake him on the inside.

'Well, you could have let him go,' she ventured good-naturedly.

'I'm done with being considerate,' he huffed.

She sighed despairingly. How she loathed being in the car with him. She always tried to decline his offer to drive her to the shops but he keeps insisting on accompanying her, arguing that if there was no parking space, he could just wait in the car rather than her having to spend ages in search of a space somewhere. The real reason, she suspected, was that he was bored. Since his retirement a couple of years ago, he didn't seem to get out of the house much anymore.

He stopped in front of the supermarket. 'It is a good day,' he thought as he watched her striding purposefully towards the automatic doors. He put on the radio and was listening to the sports news when one of the shop assistants knocked on the car window. 'I'm sorry Mr Warren,' she said apologetically, 'I'm afraid your wife seems rather disorientated.'

'Oh, alright,' he replied. 'I'll come in.'

He found her in the baby food aisle clearly confused as to what she was doing there. He took her by the hand and led her back to the car. 'Alright, Mary,' he said, although he knew that Mary could not be reached right now, and it might be some time before she returned.

He steered his Audi towards the exit but the lane was blocked by another car reversing into a parking bay.

'Come on lady,' he moaned as he watched the woman's second attempt to back into the space. 'You could get a lorry in there!'

Once back home, he went into the kitchen to make some tea when his wife entered lamenting, 'Oh dear, we have no lemons left.'

'Not to worry,' he said reassuringly, 'I'll take you down to the shops later.'

Edgar Degas
Interior (The Rape), 1868-69

Interior

'Once, you said,' Marion hissed when she heard him lock the door.

'You only have yourself to blame. You shouldn't have made it so exciting for me,' replied Émile whilst letting his eyes glide greedily over every inch of her half dressed body.

'So you like forcing yourself on women,' she snapped.

'Only if they enjoy it.'

'Don't flatter yourself. You're mistaking repulsion for desire.'

Marion straightened up and pressed her back hard against the wall in an effort to control her shivering body. She looked at him defiantly. 'I feel sorry for you,' she said with feigned sympathy. 'It can't be easy to be so loathed.'

Émile just smiled. A steely, ruthless smile that did not extend beyond a harsh lip movement. A smile that always preceded violence. 'Do you need help undressing,' he breathed whilst advancing towards her.

'Get out,' she said angrily. 'You had what we agreed on. I didn't. But I should have known better than to trust scum like you. Now get out,' she shouted. 'There won't be a second time.'

Not deterred by her rejection, he planted himself in front of her. More than a head taller than her, he stood there imposing and threatening. Suddenly, his coarse hand grabbed the top of her undergarment and with a swift and violent movement ripped it off to expose her breasts. 'I could have you right now,' he snarled, 'but that wouldn't be much fun. I'd rather wait until you beg for it.'

He then turned around and hurried to unlock the door. As it slammed shut behind him, Marion sat down on the bed barely able to breath. She had won today, but she could not delight in her victory because she knew she was unable to defeat him, and now she was terrified of what consequences her boldness may incur.

She didn't have to wait long to find out. The following Sunday when she arrived at the Prison de la Santé for her usual weekly visit, she was refused entry. No reason was given, not that she'd expected an explanation. Émile was the prison governor and had total authority over all the prisoners as well as all the guards. Marion was powerless against Émile. As much as she hated him, abhorred him, she shouldn't have aggravated him, although she somehow preferred his wrath to his desire. She knew of course that one was as unavoidable as the other. It had felt good to repel him but she was painfully aware that she was not the only one being punished for it. She could not stand up to Émile without at the same time hurting her husband. And she certainly did not want Gustave to find out about Émile's abuse of her. After all, breaking Émile's nose in a fight to defend her honour, was what had landed him in prison in the first place. Marion was convinced that the only reason Gustave was still alive was so that Émile could use him to get to her. Marion and her husband were both at the mercy of this ruthless and vicious gaoler. And eighteen months was a long time.

Marion was expecting another visit from Émile before the week had ended. But Sunday came and there had been no sign of Émile. As always, Marion prepared a little basket of fruit and some calissons to take for her husband, despite having little hope of being admitted this time. She knew Émile would never give up. To her surprise, the prison warden let her pass without problems. She sat down on one of the stone benches in the little room which was already crowded with other visitors. Clutching her basket, nervously twisting her hands around the plaited wicker handle, she waited for the iron gates at the other end of the room to be unlocked. Marion was looking forward to seeing her husband, and she was aware that he depended on her visits for his sanity, but sometimes the pressure of cheering him up, pretending that all was fine with her, almost made her sick. She was deep in thought about the various little stories she could entertain him with when the gates opened and the rattling of shackles could be heard. Slowly, the prisoners shuffled into the visitors' enclosure. There was no sign of Gustave and Marion suspected that this was another round of Émile's cruel games. To play with people's emotions seemed to be a passion of his. She was about to get up when two guards, dragging what looked like a lifeless bundle, headed in her direction. They dropped their load right at her feet. She barely recognised him. His face was a bloody and swollen mess. Marion knelt down next to her husband, her tears mingling with the blood that continued to ooze out of his multiple wounds. When she touched his arm, he flinched. That was the only response she got from him. He couldn't talk, he couldn't move. She took out a handkerchief and lightly dabbed at his wounds. Not that it helped him or made any difference to his appearance, but she had to do something. She couldn't just sit there looking at this human being, her husband, reduced to a battered, soiled, unrecognisable mass, a broken body, a soul stripped of all dignity. Gustave desperately needed help, proper medical care. And she knew there was only one way he would get that.

As she got up, she noticed Émile standing triumphantly just behind the iron gate. She walked up to him. 'Please,' she whispered, 'I beg you.'

He smiled at her, that same vicious, contemptuous grin that always sent a shudder down her spine, before commanding the guards to bring a stretcher and take the injured prisoner to the hospital.

Émile, assured that he had finally got through to Marion, took full advantage of his power. When Marion returned from hospital where she was told that her husband's injuries were severe, yet not life threatening, she found Émile stretched out on her bed. The landlord, unable to refuse, had handed Émile a spare key to her bedsit. Marion had to beg all night for Émile's 'favour' which left her bruised and aching for days. From then on, Émile came and went as he pleased. Sometimes he stayed the whole night, other times he left after an hour, probably to find more amusement elsewhere.

It took a long time before Gustave could speak again, due to his fractured jaw. When he did, his words were not those of a loving husband but rather those of an angry one. Whilst he was lying there unable to move or talk, Émile had visited him and told him how much he was enjoying his wife, how compliant Marion had become. Now Gustave demanded to know the whole truth. Despite still being too weak to get up or even to shout, his reverberating anger oozed out of every pore, and his snorting speech, no more than a whisper really, scared Marion more than even Émile could ever achieve. She couldn't tell him the truth. Instead, she told him that Émile had lied to him because he was furious that she had refused him, which was, she assumed, also the reason why Emile had him beaten up. As she unfolded one lie after another, she felt Gustave was calming down until eventually he breathed normally again. But before she left, he hissed, 'I'd rather be beaten to death than have him touch you. Do you hear me?'

'I know,' she whispered.

She pleaded with Émile not to visit Gustave, not to tell him about their arrangement, totally omitting her knowledge that he had already done so. He finally agreed to it, but only until Gustave was fully recovered.

'The moment Gustave Delamare returns to his prison cell,' Émile told Marion, fixing his gaze on her to observe her reaction whilst his hands violated her naked body, 'we shall tell him the truth, you and I together. He has to know that he can only ever have you again when I'm done with you.'

Gustave's initial recovery was slow but after a few weeks, Marion noticed an almost daily improvement, and it terrified her. There wasn't much time left before her husband would be sent back to prison.

If Gustave found out about her and Émile, he would kill Émile and hang for it, and he would never forgive her. She had to find a way of preventing this. Luckily, Émile had stopped inquiring about her husband's health although he knew that she was visiting the hospital regularly. She also noticed that Émile wasn't quite as rough with her lately. One Sunday, after her return from hospital, he'd even asked her to accompany him on a walk along the Seine. Not daring to refuse any of his wishes or suggestions for fear of what vile reaction it may unleash in him, she accepted. It turned out to be a pleasant day. The early spring sun was warm and soothing, and Émile seemed different out there in the open, fresh air. He asked about her job as a seamstress and whether she liked the work. He talked about his childhood, his mother's early death. He was content and relaxed, he appeared human. She had not seen that side of him before. When they walked side by side along the river bank in glorious sunshine, there was none of that seediness that always accompanied his visits to her lodging. He walked next to her, keeping a respectful distance. There was no secret touching, no sudden grabbing. They stopped at a little café near the busy Pont Neuf and sat outside watching lovers and families stroll past as they delighted in the view of the river and its colourful little boats. As the afternoon sun started to fade, he accompanied her home, but not to her room. He took leave outside, bowing politely.

When Marion arrived at the hospital ward the next evening, she was shocked to see Gustave limping towards her. 'Surely,' she addressed him with some alarm, 'you are not well enough to be out of bed?'

'According to the prison governor, I am. In a couple of days I'll be transferred back to prison.'

'The governor is not a doctor,' she snapped. 'Your injuries are not yet healed. I can see in your face that you are still in pain.' She almost added that she would talk to Émile but stopped herself before blurting it out in her anger. Instead she suggested imploring the doctor for help.

'No!,' he replied sharply. 'I'll be ok.'

Marion was sick with worry. She knew that the day of Gustave's full recovery was approaching rapidly and that his eventual return to prison was inevitable, but not in *two* days. And not before he was fully fit. She was also furious with Émile. Just when she thought she had got a glimpse of his human side, the beast in him came to the forefront again. She paced up and down in her room, eagerly awaiting Émile's visit that night. When he had still not arrived by midnight, she went to bed resolute to pay him a visit the next day. She needed to talk to him before Gustave was supposed to leave the hospital because, whatever it took, she could not let that happen. She didn't know for how long she'd been asleep when she awoke feeling Émile's hands glide over her body, stroking and caressing it. It wasn't unpleasant. Gently, he pulled her towards him and she melted into his strong, muscular, naked body. He kissed her so tenderly that she forgot her hatred, forgot who he was. For once, they were just man and woman, sharing a moment of mutual desire, in search for comfort and relief.

Émile got up early and, already fully dressed, sat on the edge of the bed when she opened her eyes. The harshness of the morning light was a stark reminder that the wrong man had been sharing her bed.

'You cannot send Gustave back to prison yet,' she burst out.

'Why not?' he asked without seeming surprised by her demand.

'Because he is not well yet. He is still in pain. His fractures haven't healed properly yet. He couldn't possibly cope with the harsh prison life,' she pleaded passionately.

'But he is well enough to know the truth. Maybe I'll let him stay in hospital a little while longer but either way, you and I are going to visit him together tomorrow.'

'To do what?' she snapped. 'Break his heart? It's not enough that you have broken every bone in his body? Why do you hate us so much?'

'Your husband has to know about us. We shall tell him the truth.'

'The truth?!' she suddenly shouted. 'What is the truth, Émile? That you have forced yourself on me repeatedly? That you have threatened to hurt him if I didn't oblige you? That I abhor you? That I have hated every second you were near me …?!'

'Tomorrow,' he said icily and left.

When she arrived at the hospital the next day, scared and nervous, she found her husband lying on the bed. Apparently, Émile had sent message that the changeover was not going to take place that day after all.

'Why?' she hissed.

'I don't know,' he replied surprised at her anger.

'I tell you why!,' she burst out. 'Because he enjoys scaring and torturing people!'

'I thought you'd be pleased that I can remain here for a little longer?'

'For today,' she sighed in frustration. 'But what about tomorrow? Or will it be the day after tomorrow? He wants to keep us guessing and worrying because he likes the torture more than the kill.'

'Marion, please,' pleaded Gustave, 'don't be upset, it's exactly what he wants. Come, sit with me and tell me if the chestnut trees at the bottom of our road have started to bloom.'

As she made her way back home, Marion regained a level of calmness which enabled her to think more clearly about Émile's change of mind. She was relieved of course, for Gustave's sake as much as her own. But in some way she felt regret that her secret wasn't finally out in the open. She was exhausted from pretending to Gustave that all was well. Exhausted from living with Émile's threats, the constant fear of discovery. Yes, a part of her had longed for it to be over. And suddenly it occurred to her, that that was exactly what it would have been if Émile had turned up today and confronted Gustave with the truth – over, for everybody including Émile. The moment Gustave would learn what was going on between his wife and his gaoler, Marion would be free. Gustave would want nothing more to do with her – Émile would lose a rival, she a husband. But most of all, Émile would lose her because he would have no more hold over her. Marion realised that Émile must have come to that same conclusion and had decided that he was not yet finished with her. By the time she arrived home, she was however resolute that she would put an end to it by telling Gustave herself.

She wasn't surprised to find Émile waiting for her. He stood by the open window and only turned around when she started to speak.

'Why not today?' she asked.

He did not answer. He just looked at her, searching her face until her eyes finally met his.

'What made you change your mind?' she inquired more forcefully.

Their eyes still locked, he moved slowly towards her. When he was only an arm length away, he suddenly stopped. 'Because I have realised,' he whispered, 'that you will never really be mine if you don't want to be. So I set you free, Marion. And your husband will not have to go back to prison after his release from hospital'.

As he walked past her to head for the door, she flung her arms around him.

'Don't thank me,' he said whilst trying to distance himself from her. 'I'm only being kind to myself,' he smiled at her. 'You're too much trouble, your obstinacy is driving me crazy'. He flung his key to her room onto the bed and left.

Marion couldn't make sense of it. Nor did she know why she had embraced Émile, but it certainly wasn't to thank him. Not that he didn't deserve to be thanked for this apparently noble gesture, it just hadn't occurred to her. She should be grateful and relieved, but she was neither. A few months ago, she would have been ecstatic, now she didn't even feel a tinge of happiness. Maybe, she argued, it was that she just didn't trust Émile's sudden kindness. Still, she arrived at the hospital the next day displaying her best smiling face and pretending to be full of joy.

'What did he want in return?,' asked Gustave through clenched teeth.

'Nothing,' Marion stumbled, not having expected this reaction.

'Don't make things worse by lying,' he snapped. 'What was the price for my freedom?'

'Nothing, I swear! I was as surprised as you …'

'Oh, how touching,' he sighed, 'Émile the monster was suddenly miraculously transformed into a selfless specimen of human kindness.'

He leapt out of bed and shuffled, as fast as his shackles allowed it, up close to his wife. Grabbing hold of her hair with one hand, he pulled back her head whilst placing his other hand around her throat.

'Marion, Marion,' he whispered shaking his head. 'I am going to kill him. But what shall I do with you? Do I want somebody who so readily uses her body as a bargaining tool?,' he sneered contemptuously whilst pushing her away from him.

'But … I didn't,' she stammered knowing that it was what she had done all along to keep him safe, except this time; she did not pay for his freedom. She would never have dared to ask such an enormous favour of Émile, because when Gustave still mattered more than anything else in the world to her, she was afraid that in return for her husband's freedom, Émile might have asked her to never see Gustave again. And then, that price would have been too high. 'Strange,' she thought, 'how values change.'

'Please, Gustave,' she begged, 'don't ...'

'Does he mean so much to you now,' he interrupted her angrily, 'that you are pleading for his life? There was a time when you would have liked nothing more than to see him dead.'

'What would be the point? You'd end up in prison again rather than ...'

'You are right, defending your honour landed me in prison in the first place. Well,' he started to laugh, 'he proved me wrong after all. Maybe he was right even then.'

'Insult me as much as you want,' she said coldly, 'but think carefully about your next move and let not anger guide your decisions. We can still try to have a happy life,' she continued pleadingly, 'let's not ruin this chance. Let's leave the past behind where it belongs and embrace the future … a future together'.

Slowly, Gustave made his way back to his bed. Before lying down on it he turned around and looked at her with utter disgust, 'Get out!' he demanded.

Marion left the hospital, terrified by Gustave's threats. There was no knowing what he might do in his anger. She was upset, hurt, although not surprised that his rage was greater than his love for her. She had to see Émile. It was already late by the time she arrived at Émile's residence - a little apartment on the first floor, and part of the prison building. She had never been there before, never been invited. Hesitantly she knocked on the door. He opened almost instantly. To say he was surprised to see her would be an understatement. He was so taken aback at the sight of her that he just stood there not knowing what to do.

'Will you let me in, please,' she urged him. 'Gustave's gone crazy. He wants to kill you.'

'Why,' he asked. 'Because I decided to set him free?'

'Because he thinks I have given myself to you in return for his freedom.'

Émile only laughed in response which made Marion furious. She pushed him out of the way and entered his apartment. He quickly followed her and closed the door. Marion was surprised how homely the place looked, really comfortable and orderly. There was a leather sofa against one wall alongside a writing desk, a large armchair by the window with a little table by its side. A big gas lamp, sufficient to illuminate the whole room, dominated the top of the desk. Heavy green chintz curtains were drawn across the width of the room and Marion assumed that his bed was hidden behind them.

'Why are you here?' asked Émile.

'You can't free Gustave. Not yet. Keep him in hospital where he is safe, but still as a prisoner … until he's calmed down.'

Émile shook his head in disbelief. 'I have authorised his release. In three days' time, your husband is a free man.'

'And *you* will be a dead man!' Marion shouted hysterically.

'Then *you* should be happy,' he replied light heartedly.

'You cannot let him out!' she pleaded whilst pushing her hands angrily against his chest.

He got hold of her wrists and held them firmly. 'What do you want me to do? Have him beaten so he has to remain in hospital, and when he's recovered from that, have him beaten anew? You cannot beat the anger out of somebody. Yes, I could prevent Gustave from acting on it by prolonging his imprisonment but not forever; and during every minute, every hour of his incarceration his anger would grow.'

Of course Marion didn't want Gustave to suffer more. She wanted him to be free … but not when his mind was set on revenge; because his anger tied her to him, and she wanted to be free herself.

Émile let go of her arms. He looked at her worried face, her pained expression and smiled at her broadly, 'I never thought I'd see the day when you would be worried about my life,' he chuckled.

'I'm worried about Gustave's life, not yours,' she huffed, annoyed by his jocularity. 'If he kills you, he'll hang; and he doesn't deserve that.'

'Nor does he deserve your loyalty. As far as I am concerned, your husband is a very lucky man.'

Marion looked at him aghast. 'It's the least I can do for him.

After all it is because of me that he ended up in prison in the first place.'

'What?' exclaimed Émile in disbelief. 'How did you come to that conclusion?'

'Although I didn't do anything wrong, he fought you in defence of my honour and ...'

'Is that what he told you!?,' Émile burst out. 'My fight with Gustave had nothing to do with you. I deliberately provoked him and let him hurt me to provide me with a reason to lock him up because I was unable to punish him for the real crime he had committed.'

Utterly confused, Marion slumped down on the sofa. 'I don't know what you are talking about. What, apart from breaking your nose, was Gustave supposed to have done?'

'You really don't know,' stated Émile totally surprised by this discovery.

'Gustave had an affair with Eloise, my best friend's wife. Eloise had fallen madly in love with Gustave and, having been led to believe that Gustave felt the same way about her, she confessed to Francois, her husband, telling him that she had decided to leave him. But Gustave had no intention of leaving you, even after Eloise told him that she was carrying his child. Forlorn and destitute, she came to see me. I found her some lodging on the outskirts of town and promised to try and help. After that, I went straight to Francois' house to find him torn between grief and rage. I didn't tell him where his wife was, only that she was safe. Two days later, when I returned to my friend's house, I found their dead bodies. Eloise must have returned to try and talk to Francois, maybe ask his forgiveness ... we shall never know. He had shot her first and then took a bullet himself. But I thought you knew all that,' Émile sighed. 'And I could not understand how you were able to forgive him. That's why I hated you too ... in the beginning.'

He sat down next to her where they remained in silence for a long time. When she finally turned her pale face towards him, she looked at him with pleading eyes. 'Forgive me,' she whispered.

He gently took her hand. 'I had forgiven you even when I still thought that you had been aware of your husband's character, I forgave you … when I fell in love with you.'

When Marion confronted her husband, he tried at first to deny it all and accuse Émile of lying, but when he realised that Marion did not believe his protestations to be genuine, he eventually admitted to everything. She told him that, although she believed that he deserved to spend the rest of his life in prison, Émile had decided to set him free providing that neither she nor Émile would ever have to set eyes on him ever again. Within an hour, Gustave was transported back to prison. A few days later, standing at Émile's apartment window, Marion and Émile watched Gustave walk out of prison and disappear from their lives forever.

Caravaggio
The Cardsharps, c. 1594

The Cardsharps

'Look,' whispered Marsilio to his young companion whilst nodding towards the entrance of the taverna, 'our next customer'. Lorenzo, who had been half asleep straightened up from his slouching position and grinned at the older man. 'You think so?' he asked eagerly. Marsilio reached across the table for the pack of cards. Slowly, he started to shuffle them. 'Let's welcome the young stranger with a drink.'

Giovanni, pleased to have solid ground under his feet again, dropped his bag and took off his sea-worn cloak before advancing further into the room. His garments were made from exquisite cloth and were richly decorated. He was delicately limbed and his posture and fine features carried with them an aristocratic air. The journey from Venice had been an arduous one and had taken longer than he'd expected. In Genoa, he had to wait several days before a ship was ready to sail to Naples. And the rough sea had almost prevented arrival at his destination altogether.

'Young Sir!' called out Marsilio whilst putting the pack of cards down again. 'You look in need of some refreshment. Come and join me and my nephew, we are always glad to share a cup of wine with a deserving traveller, accompanied by good advice about the habits of our town.'

The Venetian youth hesitated, but as he looked around and could see no other table occupied he replied, 'Most kind, good sir, but let me entreat you to allow me to purchase a carafe of wine and invite you and your nephew to be my guests.'

The conversation flowed well, as did the wine. Lorenzo, being of a similar age to the stranger, took a keen interest in Giovanni, enquiring about his parentage, whence he had come from and what his plans were for the future. It became obvious that Giovanni was not just new in town, he was also a very inexperienced traveller, as well as an unpractised drinker. Marsilio, in the meantime was weighing up the young man's wealth - his attire looked extravagant, made from silk and the finest lace, and the leather pouch attached to his belt seemed full and heavy.

After insisting on paying for the next jug of wine, Marsilio offered to teach Giovanni a card game which, he pointed out, served as popular entertainment in these parts of the world. He assured the young man that it would be to his benefit to be able to play if he had any interest in getting acquainted with some of the well-to-do local folk. The youth, by now quite merry from the wine, was very keen on the idea and grateful to Marsilio for his kindness. Being an intelligent fellow, Giovanni mastered the gist of the game after only a few hands. Cheered on by Marsilio's and Lorenzo's praise, the youth let himself be persuaded to start playing for money.

'It makes a player more ambitious to win, which in turn makes the whole game more interesting,' stated Marsilio excitedly.

'Without the involvement of money,' elaborated Lorenzo, 'the game might as well be banished to a nursery'.

So the refreshments were quickly moved out of the way, now that the game was going to be more serious.

After winning the first few rounds, Giovanni was hooked. The combination of being naïve and inebriated had rendered him oblivious to the cardsharps' treachery, and so with every losing hand he hoped, strongly encouraged by Marsilio and Lorenzo, that his luck would change and he would win the next one. He did occasionally recoup some of his money but, alas, his losses far outweighed his winnings. The realisation, when he tried in vain to retrieve another gold coin from his pouch, that he had lost everything, shook the youth to the core. Marsilio generously bought Giovanni another cup of wine and paid the innkeeper to let the Venetian spend the night in the inn.

Once outside, the cardsharps congratulated each other on their success and Marsilio praised his young apprentice for his skilful performance. He then gave Lorenzo his share of the night's winnings before parting company. 'We'll meet in Arturo's taverna tomorrow,' instructed Marsilio as he was walking away.

Lorenzo too had started to put some distance between himself and the inn but, after a few minutes, he stopped in his stride. He felt sorry for the Venetian youth who'd reminded him so much of himself, when he had first arrived in Naples many months ago – so innocent, so trusting, and full of excitement and good will. Marsilio, after having cheated him out of all his possessions, had then offered him a livelihood by becoming his partner. It is easy to corrupt the destitute. Lorenzo suddenly felt ashamed of having become such an untrustworthy individual and envied Giovanni his innocence. But what would become of the youth now? As Lorenzo pondered all this, a plan started to develop, almost by itself, in his head. He never did like the mean and violent Marsilio who always took advantage of him, never paid him his full share. He hurried back to the tavern where he found Giovanni almost exactly how they'd left him, still staring at the cup in front of him, except by now the cup was empty.

'Giovanni,' he said, 'what happened to you tonight touches me deeply. You were horribly wronged, and I'm partly responsible for that.' He then confessed to the young Venetian how they had cheated him. 'But if you are willing to assist me,' Lorenzo concluded, 'I have a plan to retrieve all your money.'

Giovanni listened attentively to Lorenzo's idea, and eventually agreed to it, after Lorenzo passionately argued that it wouldn't be stealing as the money had not been obtained fairly.

'Come,' Lorenzo urged, 'we have to act quickly. And bring your belongings because I think it best for both of us to disappear afterwards. Marsilio is a violent man and quick with the knife.'

When the two young men arrived at Marsilio's lodgings, Giovanni crouched down underneath the window whilst Lorenzo hammered against the wooden panels with his fists and lamented, 'Help! Marsilio, help!' until Marsilio flung open the shutters by which time Lorenzo had run to the door and, repeating his cries for help, banged against it as hard as he could. Marsilio, leaving the window wide open, staggered to the door in his drunken stupor (because, as usual, he had carried on drinking after taking leave of Lorenzo). The moment Marsilio appeared in the open door Lorenzo grabbed hold of him, crying, 'Marsilio, oh Marsilio, I'm dying! I have to show you where I've hidden my savings for I want you to have it all. But hurry, for I fear I shan't last much longer!'

Confused as he was, the prospect of money sparked enough interest in the greedy drunkard to be dragged away by his partner. And whilst he was compos mentis enough to fumble for the key that hung at his hip to lock the door, he did not remember to close the window.

Seeing the two shadows stagger away, Giovanni climbed through the open window and searched for his money under the bed, where Lorenzo had suspected it would be hidden. There, amongst some straw and filthy rags he found a dirty jute bag filled with his coins. He swiftly transferred the coins into his pouch and quickly left the way he had entered, anxious to join up with Lorenzo at the designated meeting point.

Lorenzo, in the meantime, had led Marsilio to a deserted area of the harbour where he'd stopped at a derelict fishing boat. 'Marsilio,' he whimpered, 'deep in the hull at its bow you will find all that's left of my winnings.'

Marsilio immediately started to tear at the rotting wood to ensure better access to the hollow of the boat's hull. Quickly and quietly, Lorenzo withdrew into the darkness. He was pleased how well his plan had worked and for once in a long time, he felt good about himself in the knowledge that he had done a decent thing.

Giovanni was in the middle of counting the coins to see how many were missing, when Lorenzo approached. At the sight of the money, Lorenzo's good intentions failed him. His life of the past few months made it impossible to withstand such temptation.

'Giovanni,' he demanded, 'hand over the money and I shall decide your share.'

'But,' replied Giovanni perplexed, 'it is mine. Though you can keep whatever Marsilio gave you when you cheated me of it.'

This annoyed Lorenzo immensely and he accused Giovanni of being ungrateful. 'Without me,' he hissed, 'you'd still be sitting in the taverna – a pauper!'

'Without you,' replied the Venetian calmly, 'I may never have lost my money in the first place. You will not cheat me a second time.'

Giovanni let the coins trickle back into the pouch, but before he could secure the pouch to his belt Lorenzo lunged at him. Unable to loosen Giovanni's grip, Lorenzo drew his dagger and was about to stab Giovanni when he heard Marsilio's booming voice behind him.

'Such miraculous recovery for someone so close to death!'

Lorenzo immediately let go of Giovanni, knowing that Marsilio posed a much greater threat, and instantly twirled round ... into Marsilio's drawn dagger.

'So you thought you could cheat me and enter into a new partnership? You little rat,' he sneered at the staggering Lorenzo.

Waving the bloody dagger in front of him, Marsilio then turned to Giovanni, 'Hand me the money. You have a new partner.'

But just as he was about to advance further towards the Venetian youth, the dying Lorenzo, gathering his last strength, threw himself at Marsilio and forced his knife into his murderer's heart. As the cardsharps collapsed next to each other, Giovanni walked away, a more experienced traveller than he had arrived only a few hours earlier.

Badrig
At The Museum, 2016 © Badrig

At The Museum

Saturday was culture day. And this week Rachel had decided to visit the stately city museum because, although having passed it many a times, she had never actually been inside. Like so many people, she too was guilty of taking the country's cultural sights for granted. She was immediately impressed by the massive atrium which was filled with the most spectacular collection of sculptures, ranging from early Renaissance to contemporary artists. As she walked through the aisles, a plaster statue of a wolf suddenly caught her eye. It was smaller than its surrounding sculptures, only about forty centimetres high, and nowhere near as elegant. It was, in fact, its pitiful state that attracted her attention. Not finely carved like the neighbouring exhibits, yet the crudely chiselled work with its skewered and slightly chipped nose and sorrowful look held a different charm. And its bashed-about appearance fitted the work's title beautifully – *Fierce Wolf, tamed.*   Rachel was mesmerised by this depiction of a majestic, wild animal which had clearly been beaten into submission.

Still immersed in inspecting the wolf sculpture closely from all sides, she became suddenly aware of a commotion barely two feet behind her. She turned around and saw a man gesturing wildly at a group of people whilst shouting that nobody should move. His back was turned to Rachel but she saw that he was holding a gun. Seconds later, a shot was fired. In sheer reflex, Rachel picked up the wolf she'd been admiring, and to the piercing sound of the security alarm she ran towards the gunman and knocked him over the head with it. As he stumbled and fell, she continued to hit him until he remained motionless on the ground amidst broken pieces of plaster.

When Rachel straightened up, still clutching whatever was left of the wolf statue tightly in her hands, she was surrounded by people. Some lamenting and wailing in disbelief, others screaming out of fear, many shouting to express their gratitude and thanking her for her bravery. A few minutes later, the museum's security guards and a few of the staff were elbowing their way through to her, commanding the gathered crowd of spectators to disperse. With horror in their eyes they took in the scene, then started yelling at Rachel to let go of the bust. So she did, shattering the already headless remains as it landed on the stone floor. There was a gasp of terror from the museum staff and Rachel began to tremble as she looked into their hostile grimaces. They pushed her against the wall accompanied by angry outbursts. 'Do you realise what you've done, you silly woman?

You've just destroyed thousands of pounds worth of art!'

'You're insane!', shouted another distraught member of staff. 'This was an Alessandro masterpiece. It's irreplaceable!'

'You will pay for the rest of your life for this,' threatened one security guard, whilst another one added, 'You should go to prison for that, you philistine!'

Rachel was relieved when the police finally arrived. The inspector in charge was an intelligent fellow. A mere glance and he had grasped the situation. 'I see,' he said gravely. 'An Alessandro.' He then turned his attention to Rachel. 'You'd better come with me young lady.'

Rachel, still in shock, was pleased to get out of there and was looking forward to a chance to explain the real circumstances of what had happened.

Once at the station, Inspector McGriffin ordered a cup of tea to be brought to Rachel before starting his investigation. He seemed very laid back. His ruddy and blotchy complexion rendered him less attractive than he believed himself to be, and his smile lost some of its charm by revealing an incomplete set of yellow teeth. But overall, his face appeared kind.

'So,' the Inspector slid the cup of tea gentle towards Rachel, 'What's your full name, love?'

'Rachel Sinclair,' she answered quietly.

'And, Miss Sinclair,' the Inspector addressed her in a friendly tone, 'What made you choose that particular sculpture?'

'What,' she asked baffled. 'Is that really important?'

'All my questions are important, my dear, otherwise I wouldn't be asking them. Would I now?,' the Inspector replied calmly and flashed his tarnished teeth.

'Oh, of course,' stumbled Rachel. 'Well, I was really taken in by that sculpture … I just couldn't bring myself to move on … I found it mesmerising. So, I'd been admiring it for a while when …'

'Ah, it was premeditated,' the Inspector interrupted slyly.

'No!,' Rachel burst out shocked at the assumption. 'It was just natural as ….'

'Natural?,' the Inspector leaned back in his chair and looked at her with raised eyebrows. 'You think it's n-a-t-u-r-a-l to knock somebody over the head?'

'Of course not,' she replied indignantly. 'I was trying to explain that it was sheer reflex that I chose that particular piece.'

'Hmm'. The Inspector had finally succeeded in dislodging a piece of meat with his finger nail that had got stuck between his incisors during an afternoon snack. 'This reflex of yours will cost you a lot of money. The museum will sue you.'

'That's ridiculous! Surely, the museum must be insured for damages?'

'Accidental damage, yes. But this was deliberate destruction.'

'It was an emergency!'

'You should have alerted the guards. Let them deal with it. Not take matters into your own hand.'

'There was no guard in sight. I had to do something. The man had a gun and was shooting.' Rachel grew more and more agitated. She jumped up and shouted, 'Peoples' lives were in danger!'

Inspector McGriffin too got to his feet. 'Please, Miss,' he reprimanded her, 'You must contain yourself.'

Rachel took a deep breath as she sat back down. 'Did anybody die?,' she asked calmly.

The Inspector hesitated. 'Two,' he finally said, then added, 'You killed one of them.'

'In defence,' she protested.

'The man attacked you?,' the Inspector asked interestedly.

'Not me, other people. He had his back to me but I heard the shot, saw his gun ...'

'He had his back to you?,' interrupted the Inspector alert at this new piece of information. 'Did you ask him first to drop his gun before you hit him?'

'Erm, well ... no. I only thought I had to make him stop shooting ... so I hit him over the head as hard as I could.

'As hard as you could,' repeated the officer slowly. 'I see. Hmmm.' He jotted some things down in his little notebook. 'Were you aware of the value of the sculpture?'

'No! I didn't think ...'

'Hm, thoughtless vandalism,' mused the Inspector.

'How can you call it vandalism,' she shouted angrily. 'I saved lives! If I hadn't stopped him, more people would have been shot and ...'

'Actually,' the Inspector cleared his throat, 'I doubt that. He was a bad shot, very bad shot.'

'He managed to shoot one person, he could have ...'

'Well,' again the Inspector cleared his throat before he explained, 'He didn't shoot the woman per se, she died of a heart attack which may or may not have been caused as a result of seeing the gun or hearing the shot.'

'There was blood ... people screaming in agony.'

'People often scream in anticipation,' the Inspector declared dismissively. 'Seen it many a times. All it takes is for one to start and bang!,' he clapped his hands together, 'and you have a mass hysteria.'

'But I saw the blood on the floor,' Rachel protested.

'Oh that, yeah, somebody did get shot in the foot ... an accident, no big deal. So you see, Miss Sinclair, you had no reason to intervene, no reason at all.' He shook his head gravely, 'I'm afraid there is no evidence with which I could appease the museum. Are you a wealthy woman?'

Rachel could take no more of this. She pushed her cup of tea across the table, spilling its remaining contents all over the Inspector's desk. 'The man was shooting!,' she yelled. 'It was sheer luck that he didn't kill anybody! And you are asking me if I'm wealthy? Do I look wealthy?,' she screeched. 'Look at me! See these worn out shoes?' She took off her shoes and flung them on the desk right in the middle of the tea puddle, causing the Inspector to jerk back in his chair to avoid being splashed. 'Does that indicate wealth to you?!'

The Inspector quickly called for reinforcements and in a combined effort they fitted the raving Rachel with handcuffs. 'I urge you to calm down this instance,' said the inspector sternly, 'otherwise I shall have to lock you up until you do.'

A young girl had appeared to mop up the mess on the desk when the telephone started to ring. Whilst answering it, the inspector gestured to Rachel to sit back down. He smiled at Rachel as he replaced the receiver. 'That was the hospital. The gunman isn't dead after all, just concussed. Well,' he mumbled as he crossed out some of his notes, 'that cancels the murder charges'.

He took out a set of keys from the desk drawer and unlocked Rachel's handcuffs. 'You can go now,' he said, clearly having lost interest in her.

'What about the museum,' Rachel asked confused.

'Oh yes, that … erm that's a case for lawyers. No need to detain you here. Goodbye.'

Totally perplexed by the whole ordeal and her sudden release, Rachel staggered out of the police station. She was worried sick about being sued by the museum, knowing that she would never be able to pay even a fraction of what the sculpture was worth. She spent the next two weeks in a constant frenzy, scared to look at the post, until one Saturday morning the dreaded letter with the museum's purple logo finally arrived in her letterbox.

She didn't open it straight away, she simply couldn't. But after staring at it for a while, she decided to get it over with. The letter was phrased in such a convoluted manner that she had to read it twice to get the gist of it. Apparently, the statue …

'… one of the purest examples (and as such of the utmost rarity) of the unparalleled talent of the early Renaissance sculptor known only as Alessandro, was one of the most important artefacts in the museum's collection. And it was due to its immeasurable value that discussions took place some years ago about whether it might be

better to display a modern replica of the wolf whilst the 15th century original was being safely stored in the museum's secure vaults. After some deliberation, the motion gained favour across all authority with the result that implementation was finalised early last year when an exquisite replacement of the sculpture was produced, bearing such acute likeness to the original that left experts agonising over the works' identity.

There was a footnote in small print at the bottom of the page declaring that the museum would have another copy made by one of the art students, and there would be no claim for compensation.

Giulio Rosati
Harem Dance, c. 1887

Harem Dance

Orientalism wasn't really her thing, and if one of her friends hadn't helped to curate the exhibition, Susan wouldn't have bothered to see it. Still, it was quite amusing to look at these male fantasies of exotic scenes. As she looked bemusedly at yet another depiction of a harem as imagined by a European artist who had never set foot in one, a voice behind her asked, 'Do you like it?'

She turned round to take a look at the stranger who had taken the liberty of invading her privacy. He immediately apologised for startling her and explained that he simply wondered how other people perceived these painters' interpretations of countries they had never visited. He was very polite, but Susan detected a hint of cynicism behind his charming smile.

'I wouldn't say that I find the paintings particularly appealing,' she responded. 'Rather amusing and marginally interesting for a number of reasons.'

'I feel the same way about them, although, I'm certain my reasons of interest are different from yours,' he said haughtily.

'How can you be so sure?' she replied with a smile despite being slightly annoyed.

'Because my interest lies in the sheer ignorance of the Western world, which is so apparent in these paintings … and their understanding of the countries they interfere in hasn't changed much since then. Yet, they declare themselves an authority and expect to be accepted as such. It was like this hundreds of years ago and is the same nowadays.'

'Funnily enough, I do think you have a point,' she agreed.

'Oh,' he looked at her in surprise. A second later, he bowed deeply before introducing himself, 'Ameen bin Khalid'.

'Susan Bradley,' she said confidently whilst reaching for his hand, ready to grip and shake it firmly, but he quickly turned it and brought it up to his mouth to place a barely tangible kiss on it. She couldn't help but smile at this, what she considered old fashioned gesture but which seemed to be quite natural behaviour for him. In response to her reaction, he explained that in his culture firm handshakes were only exchanged in business transactions. 'But you are right, Miss Bradley,' he said bowing his head, 'we are in your country and should behave according to your custom'. He stretched out his hand again and this time on receiving hers, he shook it firmly, looked her in the eyes and said sternly, 'Very pleased to meet you, Miss Bradley'.

Susan found this extremely funny and laughed out loud. He looked at her feigning puzzlement for a moment before joining in her laughter. They continued to walk around the rest of the exhibition together and had much fun at the expense of these 19th and 20th century artists' imaginations. They agreed however that, whilst the works represented a fantasy world, the artists' talent could not be disputed. The vibrant colours, the intricacy of fabrics and patterns, left no doubt about the paintings' first class quality. When, just before exiting the gallery, Ameen asked her to join him for coffee, Susan did not hesitate to accept. She expected they would pop into the nearest Starbucks, but instead he hailed a taxi and asked to be taken to the Ritz, where he found no difficulty in securing a table for afternoon tea without having a reservation, and despite the couple ahead of them having been turned away because it was fully booked.

Susan, who was a confident and independent 29 year old marketing manager with a good salary and a reasonably active social life, found herself strangely taken in by Ameen. It wasn't just because he was handsome, and obviously wealthy – she wasn't that shallow, but his easy mannerism and intelligence captivated her. Ameen, the son of a Lebanese diplomat, was thirty-four, born in Beirut where he spent his early childhood until his parents sent him to a private school in America whilst they moved to Saudi Arabia. He grew up speaking three languages - Arabic, French and English, and he studied at Oxford and Harvard. After leaving Harvard, he returned to the Middle East where he now worked as an economics' advisor with a decent salary and the extra bonus of having to travel around the world. Susan, although not political herself, was fascinated by Ameen's view of the world. Referring back to the paintings they had just viewed, he argued that the Islamic world was still misunderstood by the West and, due to this lack of comprehension, the power of Islam was underestimated. He also explained, in a non-hostile way, that the hatred of Islamic extremists for Christians took roots centuries ago at the time of the crusades, when Christians tried to force their beliefs on the world. 'But Islam,' he concluded passionately, 'is now stronger and more widespread than ever before. Because Allah is powerful.'

'I think the reason why Islam is more widespread is because the Western world has become a lot more tolerant and is embracing people of different religions and cultures,' she said innocently.

'Really? I don't know how you can say that,' he protested gently without losing his calm. 'Explain to me, please, Miss Bradley, how tolerant is it to force women to show their naked bodies on the beach?'

'But you don't object to having scantily dressed, or even naked women running around a harem for the sole purpose of being sex slaves?,' she replied unable to hide her agitation.

He laughed heartily. 'It is obvious that your idea of a harem comes from the paintings we've just seen and which were only based on Western men's fantasies, not on reality. Harems don't exist for men's pleasure, they provide protection and comfort for women. And they are safe places for women where, should they wish, can show themselves as Allah has created them.'

'You call it protection, I call it imprisonment.'

'If you were familiar with the will of Allah, you would thank him for the safety. But regardless of your view of harems, no woman should be forced to show her uncovered body in public.'

'Is it kinder to force women to cover up their beauty?'

'I do think so, because it does not provoke and is therefore safer.'

'So you are saying that women in some cultures have to hide their attractiveness because men possess not enough will power and discipline to control their sexual urges.'

'Your attitude is typical of your culture,' he smiled at her, 'and I do not expect you to understand … but tolerance means to accept something even if one lacks the understanding of it. And your attack on the entire Islamic male population shows little tolerance.'

'Are you more tolerant of our ways? You are the one who has raised concerns about how women in the West dress in public.'

'It was merely an observation as part of an explanation,' he declared dismissively. 'I spend a lot of time in Christian countries without ever having molested anybody.'

'But in a Muslim country, no consideration would be given to a Christian's way of life,' she replied slightly irritated by his calm approach to refute all her arguments. 'Laws and politics differ from country to country, but on the whole the Western world is at least trying hard to eliminate racism and discrimination of any kind, and is intolerant of political incorrectness.'

'Without, excuse me Miss Bradley, much success, if I may say so,' he said very politely whilst bowing apologetically. It is public knowledge that black people are more likely to be searched by police, and also mal-treated during arrests and interrogations. I'm sure you are aware of the events that took place recently in America. But it's not just black people. Anybody who looks middle-eastern is immediately treated as a terrorist suspect. I constantly have my bags checked when I travel'.

'I'm not saying that these things don't happen anymore, just that they are being addressed and I'm sure that in future they will occur less and less. As for terrorist alerts, well, we have to be vigilant because safety must come first. I'm pleased we have all these security checks at airports although it is tedious and time consuming. Still, we all have to comply since 9/11, and everybody knows who was responsible for that!'

'Yes,' he answered quickly, 'the Americans'.

'You seriously believe that,' she said shocked by his conviction.

'It's common knowledge, even if not officially *acknowledged*'. He leaned towards her conspiratorially. 'It's all political game playing. Trust me, I know, I'm closely involved with world politics.'

Susan decided she couldn't argue against his claim of insider knowledge. Besides, she was getting bored talking politics, a subject she never had much interest in. 'Well, I have to admit, I'm not particularly interested in politics so don't know much beyond news headlines,' she capitulated, 'or any intelligence I get from paintings,' she quipped'.

'And that's highly informative and reliable,' he laughed. 'But seriously, don't believe everything you read in the papers'.

Ameen then inquired about her job and her family. Susan, grateful for the change of topic, told him that she was born and bred in England. The only child of middle-class parents, she had enjoyed years of private education before securing a university place at Cambridge to read English. Two years ago, when her parents decided to retire to the country, she had put down a deposit on a flat in Central London.

She still saw her parents one weekend a month when she'd either visited them or they'd come to stay with her in London, and of course she would spend Christmas with them. Ameen listened attentively as Susan rambled on about her childhood, her job, her hobbies. He nodded when needed, laughed when expected to. He made Susan feel interesting, because he made her believe that he was hanging on every word she spoke. And, apart from politics, they appeared to have a lot of common interests. When Susan finally decided that it was time to leave, she happily accepted Ameen's suggestion to follow up this extremely enjoyable afternoon with dinner, which was arranged for the next day. They dined at a Lebanese restaurant where Susan had one of the best meals ever. It was also one of the nicest evenings she had had in a very long time, and the beginning of a very passionate relationship.

Due to his charm and wit, Ameen proved a huge success with Susan's friends and ultimately, after an initial period of caution and worry about the difference in cultures, also her parents. Since their first meeting, politics had never again been discussed, relevant headlines barely even mentioned. After a couple of months, during which Ameen travelled back and forth, Susan decided it was silly that he should reside in a hotel whilst in London when he was spending all his time with her anyway. Ameen was thrilled and admitted that the thought had occurred to him too, but he didn't feel he could suggest it. It was a big step for both of them, almost like moving in together, except that he was usually only around at weekends, and some weeks not even that. Susan quickly realised that she knew nothing about Islam and that she was totally ignorant to its laws and customs. When Ameen first produced his prayer mat, she was slightly bemused but refrained from commenting as she didn't want to offend him and, after a while she got used to it. Similarly with food. In the beginning it was no problem because they were eating out all the time but the first time she cooked for him, he refused to touch the meat and only dined on dry bread, salad and plain vegetables – a traditional roast dinner was clearly a fauxpas.

He explained about halal food, and why it played such an important part in his life. 'Surely,' he asked, 'you must have some dietary disciplines in your religious doctrine?'

'Not on a permanent basis, but there is some fasting, like Lent, for instance, when Christians are not supposed to eat meat. But I'm not religious,' Susan replied, sounding almost apologetic.

'Because you were brought up with the wrong religion, a religion that does not teach you respect and decency,' he said gravely.

'I think any religion, the moment you believe in it, will make you respectful of and decent to others. The main problem is not the religion but whether you believe or not.'

'But it is in your god's hands to make you believe, and your god has failed.'

'To believe that, you'd have to first accept his existence. I do envy you in a way … your strong conviction that you always have somebody to lean on, that everything, no matter how bad, is god's will and therefore must have a purpose.'

'I don't know how you can get through life without it. But,' he hesitated, 'maybe you are not supposed to. Maybe, the reason why we met is so that I can show you the way to … to the all-seeing, all-knowing, almighty Allah.'

'Let's not make unrealistic assumptions,' Susan laughed. 'I've done very well so far without believing in anything but common sense. And you don't mind that I'm a nontheist, do you?'

'I'm not sure. I didn't at first … but now that … well, what I'm trying to say is that … erm,' he took hold of her hands and kissed them, 'it's different now … because I'm in love with you.'

It was the first time he had told her that he loved her and Susan was ecstatic. She threw her arms around him and whispered 'I love you too.'

After that, nothing was mentioned anymore about religion until a few weeks later when Susan expressed her wish to meet Ameen's parents. She was shocked when told that this would be impossible unless she embraced the Islamic faith. His parents, being devout Muslims, would never accept an infidel into their home.

'But,' she protested, 'my parents have taken you in with open arms.'

'It just shows the lack of their faith,' he replied rather arrogantly.

Susan was outraged by his insensitive remark, and the issue of parental love versus love for god versus love between man and woman, escalated into their first, and full-blown argument which resulted in Ameen fleeing the scene and leaving Susan in floods of tears. Ameen did not return for several weeks, nor did he ring during this absence. Susan was devastated. She couldn't bear the thought of never seeing him again, but her numerous calls remained unanswered. When he finally re-appeared, without prior announcement, one Saturday morning, he asked Susan to marry him. She was so delighted to see him that she agreed without hesitation, without giving any consideration to their differences in culture, religion, politics. He said he had taken three weeks off work and had thought that they could be married during this time.

Susan's parents, having secretly hoped that their daughter's affair with Ameen had come to an end, were devastated by the unexpected news and did not pretend otherwise. They warned Susan that a union of such diverse cultures and religions was too complex to overcome. 'And where would you live,' they asked, worried that Ameen might insist on moving near his parents which, of course, would mean that Susan would have to convert to Islam. They urged their daughter to find out about Ameen's intentions before rushing into marriage.

Susan was annoyed about her parent's lack of enthusiasm. And whilst she understood their concerns, she also felt that they could still show some support for her happiness. Besides, they should trust her judgement. After all, she wasn't a love-sick teenager, she was an intelligent woman who wouldn't just take off into an unknown world on a whim. Of course, she expected that she would have to make an effort to at least understand Ameen's religion, but she was convinced that he would not insist on her converting. And nothing whatsoever had been mentioned about leaving England. They loved each other, the rest therefore could be worked out. Ameen re-assured her that he would never force her into something she did not want to do and insisted that they should enjoy the weekend before entering into discussions about boring details.

Early Monday morning, Ameen declared that he had to run some errands and that he would be gone for most of the day. Susan took the opportunity to meet with a friend for some preliminary wedding dress viewing. They visited three major department stores and Susan noted down details of several dresses she'd liked. Intelligent as she was concerning many things, Susan lacked an understanding regarding religious passion in other cultures because firstly, she was a self-proclaimed atheist and secondly, she strongly believed that the reason why multi-cultural societies existed at all, was due to the mutual tolerance they showed each other. That's why she was so impressed when Ameen, during their first meeting, expressed the true meaning of tolerance as accepting something, even if we fail to understand it, just because it is important to others. And if it worked for whole societies, then surely it would work between two individuals who not only both believed in that same concept but also loved each other.

Later that evening, Susan learned that Ameen had been to see an imam who was prepared to marry them providing Susan would accept the laws of Allah. Susan was shocked and incensed that Ameen hadn't mentioned his intention before he went out. In the discussion that followed, she protested that she was not willing to convert to Islam, but accepted that Ameen would never set foot inside a church and thus suggested that they should only have a civil ceremony in a registry office. That way, nobody had to compromise. But Ameen argued that that would be unfair as she, by admission, wasn't religious whereas his faith was very important to him. He assured her that he did not expect her to change in any way, he just wanted her to keep an open mind, to show a willingness to understand what was such a vital part of his life. It became clear that Ameen was not willing to compromise when it came to his faith. If Susan wanted to become his wife, it would have to be in a Muslim ceremony. Worn down by arguments and swayed by her love, she eventually agreed. In return, he promised her a civil wedding after they had been united before Allah. Happy about the satisfactory result of their wedding plans, Ameen handed Susan a package with the words, 'A token of my love and my gratitude for bowing to my wishes'. As she unwrapped the hand-painted reproduction of *Harem Dance* he added, 'It was misinterpretation that brought us together, let truth guide our future'.

Ameen had arranged for Susan to accompany him to the mosque a few days ahead of taking their vows before Allah. When Susan went into the bedroom the night before she was due to meet the imam for the first time, she found a chador, hijab and burqa laid out on her bed. Overwhelmed by the sight of it, she ran out of the room sobbing. She suddenly remembered all the beautiful white wedding dresses she had seen, remembered the festive church weddings she had been to with the joyful dancing and celebrating afterwards – all of that she was happy to forgo … in favour of a simple civil ceremony, but not for that. Not for a nun's habit, a mourning cloak, because that's what it represented to her. She could not see the beauty Ameen saw in the garments, could not share the pleasure he so obviously felt by merely imagining her wearing them. He tried to calm her but Susan was inconsolable, and seeing his smiling, happy eyes being taken over by painful sadness made her cry even more. He took the framed copy of *Harem Dance* off the wall, packed quietly and left without another word.

A few days later Susan received a postcard of Rosati's *Harem Dance* with the words scribbled on the back: *Victims of misinterpretation.*

Thomas Gainsborough
Conversation In A Park, 1720

Conversation In A Park

Despite all, she was a happy soul. She could derive pleasure from simple things, like the first rays of sunshine after a rainy day. And most people who knew Lady Desiree Broadmoor would consider her very lucky indeed. Many even envied her because she was refined, sophisticated, beautiful; this was also why she was married to one of the wealthiest landowners in the country. And for a while, she too believed herself fortunate to be thus blessed.

Lord Broadmoor was the most gallant and attentive suitor any lady could wish for. Desiree was madly in love with him and couldn't wait to get married. The wedding itself was a fairy tale affair, no expense was spared, and the couple were as handsome as any prince and princess. Lord Broadmoor's long standing friend, Count Fielding, made a touching speech about love and friendship declaring that no life can be complete without them and swore his lifelong love for his friend, adding that he hoped to be allowed to extend his friendship to her ladyship. The wine flowed freely and the guests danced until the early morning hours, but Lord and Lady Broadmoor withdrew shortly after midnight.

Desiree's desire for her husband and his longed for embrace increased with every minute he kept her waiting. Lying naked in the marital bed, covered only by a thin white, transparent silk sheet, listening to the subdued rustling movements coming from her husband's dressing room, she suddenly became aware of some hushed voices. At first she assumed her husband was talking to Bernard, his valet, but then remembered he had already been dismissed for the night. Then the voices grew louder and more agitated, and whilst she could not hear what was said, there was no doubt that both voices were male. Who would annoy her husband on his wedding day? What could possibly be more important than somebody's wedding night? She was growing impatient, anxiously wondering what it would be like when he eventually took his place next to her.

The sudden forcefulness with which the door opened made her shudder but also heightened her excitement. She didn't ask about his delayed arrival, she just closed her eyes and let her body do the talking. The silk sheet clung to her body and in the light of a bright, full moon he looked at her nakedness. She was beautiful. He watched her chest move with every excited, expectant breath. When he placed his hand on her thigh, she let out a moan. He knew she'd be passionate. But her longing scared him. Gently and slowly, he pulled down the sheet until her heaving, ivory skinned body was completely exposed. As his hands touched her breasts, she wildly groped for his arms. Feeling his shirt sleeves when she was expecting bare arms, she opened her eyes and asked, 'Aren't you …,' but he stopped her by placing a finger over her lips. 'Ssh,' he whispered, and continued to let his hand slide down her writhing body until it reached its destination. Overcome by a feeling of such intensity, she let out a scream whilst pushing her hips towards him. When she regained her senses, she could feel him inside her.

Slowly she opened her eyes. Her husband, still fully dressed, removed his hand from her groin and wiped his bloody fingers in a large linen towel which he then thrust between her legs. Painfully conscious now of her nakedness and terribly ashamed of having derived so much pleasure when she had clearly given none, she clumsily started to retract the silken coverlet in order to protect her body from his cold stare. He was standing over her, impatient to leave. 'That's all I can do for you, all I can ever do for you.'

The hoarseness of his voice indicated some emotion but did not lessen the severity of the devastating statement. She was still lying there, with the coarse cloth wedged between her legs, long after he had left, feeling upset, sad and worried. Worried because she thought that she might have done something wrong. She hadn't known what to expect or what was expected of her, but she was certain it was not supposed to be the way it had happened. Once she had asked her mother if there was anything she should know about the wedding night, but her mother had made it quite clear that one did not talk about such things. She merely replied, 'Make sure you please your husband, my dear, that's all.' But when she'd protested that she wouldn't know how to, her mother blushed and, with an embarrassed laugh, told her, 'He'll show you, don't worry.'

When Desiree woke up the next morning, she was terrified of facing her husband. Never before had he looked at her so coldly as he did last night. Had she disappointed him? Did he not like what he saw when he entered the room? When she finally ventured downstairs for breakfast she was told that his lordship had gone away on business and wouldn't be back for a few days. The relief she first felt about his absence was soon replaced by anger. How dare he abandon her without explanation? If she had displeased him, then he ought to tell her the reason for the offence. Not to do so was unfair and cowardly. Desiree decided to confront her husband the moment he returned. Until then, she busied herself with adapting to her responsibilities as lady of the manor, and took pleasure in the extensive gardens she could now call her own. She thoroughly enjoyed her new role, and loved organising lunches for other well-to-do ladies, as well as hosting picnics for the parish children. She had always been very generous, especially to those less fortunate, and now she had ample means to be even more charitable.

Three weeks later, during which time she had had no communication from her husband, Lord Broadmoor returned, accompanied by his friend, Bertie Fielding. Desiree welcomed them both with a warm smile and genuinely felt joy. Her husband rewarded her with a long, passionate embrace. And Lord Fielding commented laughingly, 'I don't honestly know, Hugh, how you manage to stay absent for so long from this beautiful wife of yours!' With a wink in Fielding's direction, Hugh Broadmoor replied brashly, 'Business, old chap, has to come first. My wife will understand that.'

Desiree took pride in showing off to her husband how well she had settled into her duties, how much control she had over the whole household and how well respected she was by all. Not only that, everybody seemed to enjoy working for her, trying to please her far beyond what was expected of them. It did not escape Lord Broadmoor's attention and he quietly congratulated himself for having chosen his wife so well. And he was sure that, eventually, she would cope admirably with the unusual terms he was going to impose on their marriage.

That night, lying on the bed, Desiree waited patiently, fully dressed, for her husband. When the door finally opened, it was late morning. 'My goodness,' his voice boomed into the stillness, 'did you sleep in your clothes?' But rather than answering him, she asked sleepily, 'Where were you?'

'I had one of the other rooms made up so I wouldn't disturb you,' then added as a way of explanation, 'it got rather late last night … it usually does with Flirtie.'

'Flirtie?' she asked, puzzled.

'Fielding. It's his nickname, you didn't know? We gave it to him years ago because of his numerous female acquaintances, none of them ever leading to any serious attachment although he's been engaged several times.'

'No, I didn't know,' she said, showing no interest in continuing on that subject. 'I was hoping to talk to you.'

'Yes, … I know … we need to … erm, talk. And we shall … but not now … I have to go. Promised Flirtie a ride down to the lake. Have you been there yet? It's beautiful at this time of year.'

He was gone before she could utter a reply. During the following days Lord Broadmoor continued to devote his entire time to entertaining Bertie Fielding. And after a while, Desiree gave up waiting for her husband at night. It seemed he had permanently moved to another room. He never even dropped in to see her in the morning, and she hardly set eyes on him all day. Yet, whenever their paths did meet, usually during meal times, Hugh Broadmoor would be most charming in his display of a caring, loving husband. Desiree did not know what to make of it. She had expected that, once married, her husband would want to spend time with her, confide in her, share her bed at night. She had expected to have a happy marriage … with children, and she refused to accept anything less, although she realised that it would be up to her to bring about the necessary changes to the current situation. So the sooner she confronted her husband and found out what had displeased him, the sooner she could work on how to regain his favour.

Immediately after lunch was finished, and before the two men could disappear again for the rest of the day, Desiree, making sure at least two of the servants were present (she had realised that her husband's charm relied on an audience), declared, 'My dear Count Fielding, I hope you don't mind if I borrow my husband for a little while? Why don't you wander around the rose garden and check on my newest acquisitions. I promise my husband will be joining you anon.'

Bertie Fielding bowed politely and left the room, leaving Hugh no choice but to abide by his wife's wishes. Whilst her husband adjusted his sword, Desiree picked up her bonnet and tied the silk ribbon under her delicate chin before leading the way into the garden. She walked briskly despite her floor length silk dress which rustled in unison with the dead autumn leaves, and strode purposefully towards a wooden bench by the little pond with its charming pavilion, where she had spent many a lonely afternoon. She sat down, but before she had even straightened out her dress, she turned to him, 'What did I do wrong? How did I displease you on our wedding night that you treated me with such contempt?'

Hugh Broadmoor stopped in front of her. He was surprised by the confidence in her voice, the sharpness of her tone. He was always aware of the necessity of this confrontation, but he had been dreading it.

'It wasn't what you did … it was your expectation. I … '

'How? I didn't know what to expect. I was waiting for you to show me how I could please you.'

'You were expecting to be happy, waiting for me to make love to you.'

'How can that be wrong? You are my husband. I love you! And I understood that you loved me … that's why you married me.'

'I do love you. I think you are the perfect wife for me. I just cannot make love to you. There are different kinds of love – what I feel for you is a deep brotherly affection. I would like you to become my friend and confidant, somebody to share my joys and sorrows … my life with … just not my bed.'

Nothing could have prepared Desiree for what she had just heard. Overcome by dizziness and a feeling of nausea, she found it difficult to keep her composure. 'Why? You married me? Why can't you love me like a husband should love his wife?'

'I'm in love with someone else.'

'How could you do this? How could you pretend to love me? Propose to me? Marry me, just to break my heart? Why didn't you marry the one you really love?'

She raised her eyes to him and looked at him coldly, not transmitting any of the hurt and pain she was feeling. What he found in the depth of her eyes was strength and determination, an unwillingness to be broken. And to him, it was an indication that she would be alright. He turned his head, unable to hold her gaze any longer.

'Because it is impossible, it could never be,' he said almost inaudibly.

When Hugh Broadmoor next looked down at his young, beautiful wife, tears were freely flowing down her cheeks. She made no attempt to wipe them away, almost as if she didn't even notice that she was crying. He pitied her, and he was ashamed that he had tricked her. But he had no choice. His father's will demanded him to be married by the age of twenty-eight otherwise the whole estate would go to his cousin's family. And Desiree certainly fitted the role as Lady Broadmoor perfectly – she was charming, intelligent, beautiful, kind – if only he could have spared her feelings.

'Who? Who is standing between me and happiness,' she asked calmly, and again surprised him by how well she was able to control her emotions.

He had never had any intention of telling her the whole truth. How could he trust her to keep his secret? A secret he had guarded all his life? Yes, he had betrayed her. And yes, it was unfair. But so was his situation. He sat down next to her and retrieved from his pocket a little book of his favourite quotations.

'Thomas Fuller,' he proclaimed, 'a very wise and learned man, once said: *There is more pleasure in loving than in being beloved.*'

'That same wise man,' she replied sharply, 'also said: *A man's best fortune, or his worst, is his wife.* Which one, dear husband, would you like me to be?' And then added in a threatening tone, 'Beware, because I care not for just *playing* your wife.'

Smiling, Lord Broadmoor turned to his wife, and with a nonchalant wave of his hand, and a confidence that only status and wealth could conjure up, he declared, 'I don't think you have a choice, my darling.'

Pierre-Auguste Renoir
The Swing (La balançoire), 1876

The Swing

'No, you go first,' squealed little Michelle with delight. 'I want to see how high you can go!'

'Alright, I shall,' replied Christine, happy to please her little cousin. 'Just make sure you keep a safe distance.'

'Don't worry, I'll see to it that she does,' reassured Christine's father.

Christine was very fond of her little cousin and loved spending time with her, as did Monsieur Robard. And although he always complained that Michelle was quite a handful, he really looked forward to the girl's visits. Somehow, they always ended up at the same place in the nearby park – the swing, which Michelle insisted was her 'favourite place on earth'. And it was such a joy to watch the delight in the little girl's face when she soared into the air shouting 'Higher! Higher!' Apparently, Christine used to love being on the swing when she was that age. That's probably why she often caught her father gazing lovingly at Michelle whilst his thoughts seemed to transport him to a different world. But conjuring up happy memories from Christine's childhood, when her mother was still alive, always left a shadow of sadness in her father's eyes. Christine couldn't remember her mother anymore, she could only recall how upset she was when she died. And the funeral - she still got flashbacks of that. So much black, there was so much black that day.

Christine was so excited at the birth of her little cousin, that Monsieur Robard agreed with his sister and brother-in-law that Michelle, as soon as she was old enough, was to spend one weekend every month with him and his daughter in their luxurious apartment in the prestigious Place des Vosges, right in the centre of Paris. Now five, Michelle, as well as her hosts, had been cherishing these visits for the past two and a half years. Almost every outing ended with a visit to the swing. Monsieur Robard did not always accompany the girls, but today his daughter had been very persistent that he should. Unbeknown to her father, Christine was in a passionate relationship with a man she had met a few months ago, incidentally at this very swing, during one of Michelle's visits. She had now decided that it was time for her two favourite men to meet. So she had arranged for Philip to arrive at their usual meeting place at 2pm. The moment Christine saw Philip in the distance, she slowed down until the swing moved only gently back and forth. 'Oh Papa,' she beamed excitedly, 'what a coincidence! Here comes an acquaintance of mine.'

Monsieur Robard was always glad to meet some of Christine's friends, especially the male ones as he was sure that sooner or later one of these young men would be asking him for the hand of his beautiful daughter. So he took a step forward with his arm already half outstretched and a heartily meant 'Enchante' on his lips. Philip Arnaud too was ready to return the greeting with equal warmth. Yet, as soon as Monsieur Robard was told the other man's name, his demeanour changed and, much to the embarrassment of his daughter, he staggered back and leaned against a tree making it quite obvious that he had no interest in entering into a conversation with her friend. With a rudeness that shocked Christine, her father told Philip not to stop as he was interrupting their family afternoon. Philip had no choice but to take his leave. With a threatening side-glance at his daughter accompanied by the demand that she would never see this man ever again, Monsieur Robard turned around and started to walk away. Christine had never known her father to use such an angry tone. She quickly jumped off the swing and grabbed Michelle's hand to follow her father. 'Papa,' she stammered, 'what's wrong? Why are you so rude to my friend?'

'This despicable man is nobody's friend,' came her father's icy reply.

'How can you say that? You don't know Philip!'

'I know of his reputation with women, and it is obvious that he has no morals, otherwise, at his age, he wouldn't have befriended a young girl like you!'

It wasn't just his reaction but the fierceness with which he'd responded that made her decide to refrain from further investigation right now. Once her father had calmed down, maybe later that evening, maybe the next day, Christine would convince him to give Philip a proper chance. He had to. She loved Philip and he loved her. For the moment though, she decided it was best to let the matter rest.

But Monsieur Robard was not willing to enter into further discussion about Philip. The mere mention of Philip's name brought on the same anger in him as that day at the swing. Christine was devastated. She needed to talk to Philip. When she arrived at the arranged meeting point, Philip was already waiting for her. She threw herself into his arms, or at least that was what she had expected to do when she fell against him and put her head on his shoulder, barely able to hold back her tears. But Philip's arms did not enclose her, instead he placed them on her shoulders to hold her upright whilst he moved backwards to distance himself from her. He looked into her tear filled eyes, 'What did your father tell you?'

'He forbids me to ever see you again,' she sobbed. 'He says I'm too young and ...'

'What he really means is that I am too old,' interrupted Philip with a sinister smile. 'Well, he's right.'

'Nonsense,' she snapped dismissively ... 'but he also mentioned your reputation. What does he mean?'

'I had an affair once …'

'So?'

Philip looked anxiously at Christine, wondering how much he could tell her. 'She was a married woman.'

'Oh. Did her husband find out?'

'Yes.'

Christine seemed rather intrigued by that revelation. 'Did you break up their marriage?'

'No.'

'What happened to her?'

Philip felt suddenly annoyed at Christine's interrogation. The only reason he had even agreed to the meeting was because Robard had visited him the day before and insisted that he must end his affair with Christine, giving any explanation he wanted, as long as it wasn't the truth. It was hard though. She was so young and impressionable. He had hoped she would be shocked about his immoral affair but she seemed to find his past alluring, which of course she wouldn't, if she knew the woman's identity. But he'd rather she didn't find out. Even he was shocked when Robard told him. No wonder the old fellow reacted the way he did when meeting him at the swing. Philip still couldn't believe that he hadn't realised, not even suspected, that Christine was Danielle's daughter. How could he not have seen it? The resemblance was unmistakable.

Impatient now to bring this unpleasant conversation to an end, he ignored her question and blurted out abruptly, 'We cannot see each other again!' And then added more gently, 'Your father is right, the age gap between us is too great.'

'Philip! You cannot be serious? Papa will come round … I know he will … once he realises how much we love each other.'

He took her hands in his then bent down and kissed them. 'I'm sorry,' he whispered, 'it cannot be.'

'You are not giving up so easily. I shall not let you! My love for you is too great!'

'And mine for you too little.'

He did not mean to hurt her like this, but it seemed the only way to stop her from pursuing a hopeless situation. And whilst he did love Christine, he couldn't help wondering if it was only the close resemblance she bore to her mother, the only woman he'd ever really loved, but who was not prepared to give up her daughter for him, that attracted him to her.

Marc Chagall, *To My Betrothed*, 1911
Chagall ®/© ADAGP, Paris and DACS, London 2017

To My Betrothed

… *Whom I have adored from a distance since I first laid eyes on you, long before you even knew of my existence, and have loved from the moment we met. Whom I have worshipped more than any God could ever expect from his most devout follower. Whose body I have desired like a suffocating man desires air. No-one has, nor ever will, enchant me like you. Your charm, your wit, your beauty – perfect in all. A goddess amongst mortals.*

When you returned my love and promised to be mine, you made me the happiest man on earth – until you broke your promise and my heart.

I am compelled to write, yet know not what to say. If only I could separate my love from hate, that I could love you despite the sorrow you have caused me, and wish you well still; or could hate you without remorse and damn you for all eternity. Alas, my feelings for you combine love and hate in equal measure. It hurts to think you suffer, as much as it does to imagine you happy. One moment I wish you such evil the devil himself would be scared, and when I then think of you in great despair, I weep for you and want to rescue you from peril. Yet, seeing you happy again makes me listen to my aching heart and I start to curse you all anew.

Oh you! Who are so pure to make God proud of his creation, the truest image of the virgin, with eyes so innocent, a smile so pious. Then how can it be, that you're a whore? Moving from one to another, making the same promises, giving the same expectations … and deceiving all. Spreading your legs like Lucifer his wings on his descent to hell. Ah, but my mind plays tricks, and I don't know what's true, what's false. Are you a saint? Are you a devil? Are you both?

You filled my ears with such sweet sounds that, whenever I closed my eyes, your naked body clad only in a silken sheet, appeared like a holy apparition, tending to me alone, fulfilling all my dreams. But now, I dare not close my eyes as when I do, visions of vulgar orgies unfold wherein you tend to man and beast. Your naked body fully exposed and lusting for any vile touch. Oh, how I loathe you for inciting such illusion ... how I loathe myself for seeing you like this. The Lord has bestowed you with such pleasing looks that would put Aphrodite in the shade. Your beauty made me appear the beast. Now you are more bestial than the lecherous minotaur.

So fare you well, love inducer and destroyer. With my best wishes for a future filled with both glimpses of happiness and great despair.

Sergei Ivanovich Bogomolov put down the pen and leant back in his chair. He felt better now that he had put his true thoughts and feelings onto paper; and into better, more honest words than his three previous attempts which lay scattered across the floor. For extra reassurance he read through the letter again, flinching at some of the harsh words his tormented mind had so eagerly spat on the page, but then argued that Olga Fedorova had to know how he felt; had to be made aware of the injury done him, had to realise that she had torn apart a loving heart and had inflicted a gaping wound, and that she alone was the cause of his tortured soul. Yes, his words were indignant and condemning but it was her disgraceful behaviour that had sucked them from his pen. Sergei Ivanovich was convinced that this was the message he would personally deliver that afternoon.

But what if he should find her remorseful? Maybe she only wanted to make him jealous, to test how strong his love was? It was possible that she deeply regretted having broken off the engagement and was now heartbroken, feeling lonely and destitute. In which case he could certainly not present her with such a damning note. Back and forth he disputed this dilemma until he concluded that it was best to write a second, a kind and forgiving letter, with the intention of taking both when calling on the lady. He would be able to assess which letter was the appropriate one by the reception he received.

As he set off, armed with the two notes, each contradicting the other one's content, he placed one in the right hand and the other in the left hand pocket of his cloak. Shortly afterwards, he found himself approaching the designated residence. Through the grand bay window, he saw his beloved Olga Fedorova jump joyfully to her feet. His heart started to pound, convinced that her excitement was due to having seen him arrive. He quickly retrieved the letter declaring his eternal and indestructible love for her, from his right pocket. But just as he was about to knock on the door a man appeared in the room and, to his utmost terror, the two embraced and a second later their mouths were locked in such a passionate kiss that Sergei Ivanovich, despite his repulsion at the sight, could not take his eyes off them.

Suddenly he realised that he was holding both letters in his hand without remembering which was which. But he must not give her the wrong one! There was only one letter she deserved, and even that one he now considered to be too kind. As he agonised to identify the right letter, he panicked and inadvertently knocked on the door. He thought of running away, but the maid was too quick. Seeing the two sealed envelopes in his hand, she swiftly took both off him and shut the door as quickly as she had opened it.

Dumbfounded, Sergei Ivanovich was unable to move. How could he let this happen? Why did he not hold on to one of the letters, or indeed both, so he could have written an even more fitting one? It plagued him that he would forever be stamped a fool in her mind. Gazing through the window he glimpsed the maid presenting both envelopes on a silver tray. He held his breath as he watched Olga Fedorova reach for his ill-fated notes. She lifted both off the tray, then smiled whilst tearing them in half before letting them drop to the floor.

Hendrick Pot

A Merry Company At Table, 1630

A Merry Company At Table

'Well, gentlemen,' croaked the old hag whilst glancing meaningfully round the table, 'an even footing – something for everyone.' The three men nodded satisfactorily as they reached out to help themselves to the freshly arrived oysters which were arranged in three neat piles on a large platter. But before they had even got hold of one, she added, 'And I wasn't referring to the oysters.' At which they all laughed heartily.

After a few more rounds of wine, the conversation turned to business. 'Do you have another lady,' asked one of the men. 'Because how else would we all leave happy here?'

'My good gentleman, what do you mean,' replied the old woman feigning surprise. 'There are only three of you. I should have thought one each is quite sufficient.'

'You cannot be serious,' burst out one of the men whilst his friends looked at her in astonishment and the two young girls giggled delightedly.

'A jape,' shouted one of the men putting on a fake laugh.

'I never jest when it comes to business,' replied the old woman in earnest.

'But,' objected one of the men, 'we pay good money, and we expect to get what we pay for.'

The owner of the brothel turned her wrinkled face towards him and gave him a big toothless smile. 'You may get more than you pay for,' she said ominously. 'Do not underestimate the experience of age. After all, these ladies,' she made a sweeping gesture towards the two young girls, 'are my apprentices … and their education is not yet complete. So be wise.'

'I don't want to look upon a wrinkled face – it kills my desire,' retorted one of the men.

'Yes,' chipped in another, 'and if the face is wrinkled so is everything else.'

'Gentlemen,' said the old woman calmly, 'we all look the same in the dark.'

'Pah,' shouted the third man, 'we can still feel the difference.'

'Aye,' replied the woman cheerfully, 'especially in the pleasure you'd be receiving. Trust me, you'll all be served well. I'll promise you that. But on of you will have an exceptional and unforgettable experience, and he will be the one sending a lot more business our way to be sure. But,' she said warningly, 'you should know that this is only for proper men. I do not offer this to the young, they get too excited.' She winked at the three men, 'If you know what I mean.'

Realising the fellows' rising interest in what she was saying, she continued to fill their ears with extraordinary promises before concluding, 'Of course such service would be more expensive.' She shrugged her shoulders and looked at them questioningly. 'And maybe it would be too much ...'

'No, no, no,' they shouted in unison.

So intrigued were the men by the old woman's claim that each one of them was eager to have that special experience. They were desperately trying to convince each other to choose one of the lovely young ladies for their night's companion, and it became obvious that there was no demand for either of the pretty girls anymore. The three women listened in silence to the men arguing, the young women pretending to sulk because they were being rejected, the old hag smiling mischievously, whilst Hans, the servant, kept refilling their cups with wine.

'Now, gentlemen,' the old woman finally intervened, 'seeing that you are all determined to have the best time of your life, we shall try to accommodate you all.'

At this, the men immediately sat to attention and listened intensely to the old woman's instructions. She told them that they would be led to different rooms upstairs where they would have to wait patiently as they couldn't all be attended to at the same time, demand being so high, and one wouldn't want the quality of the service to suffer by having to rush things. The three men nodded keenly in agreement whilst uttering re-assurance that they would comply with whatever was asked of them. Once the fee was agreed and payment handed over, they were shown to their rooms, not knowing in which order they would be visited. Eagerly, they took off all their clothes and lay down naked on the bed in total darkness, just as they were instructed.

After about twenty minutes, the first door was noisily flung open ensuring the customer would at least half wake from his drunken stupor. A big, unidentifiable shape bounced into the room. This huge body then started to tickle the heavily breathing man with feathers, starting at the sole of the feet and advancing all over the body. The man shrieked so loudly that it could be heard throughout the house. As the tickling was replaced by boxing, the man's laughs turned to shouts of 'Ah! Oh!' This intermittent tickling and boxing, and the man's changing response went on for at least fifteen minutes. Interpreting this noise as sounds of pure joy, his comrades in the adjoining rooms got more and more animated at the prospect that such delight would soon be upon them. Finishing off with tickling, the enormous shape stopped suddenly to let the man catch his breath, during which time he lit a small candle and held it briefly to his head, just long enough for the man to get a glimpse of it. Seeing the monstrous head of an enormous ugly goat the man screamed as if he had glanced at the devil himself. After that, the door was flung open and shut, and all was eerily quiet.

Before entering the next room, Hans took off his goat's head and wiped his face, which was covered in sweat, with a cool, damp cloth. A few minutes later he repeated the process with the next customer, and then applied the same procedure to the third man.

The three men, scared out of their wits, and not knowing if they had all been given the same treatment, were too embarrassed to tell their story and so they all pretended that they had had the most extraordinary night (which, in a way, was true), evident, so they claimed, by the sounds of delight that could be heard from each one of them.

The old hag waited downstairs as they took their leave and enquired if everything had been to their satisfaction. They thanked her profusely and swore that it was truly the best night of their lives, and promised to send many more customers her way. Which indeed, they did, because they all had a wicked side and wanted to trick both their friends and foes.

Edward Burne-Jones, *Vespertina Quies*, 1893

Vespertina Quies

Jane had never been to Minford Hall before, despite having moved within two miles of it just over a year ago when she inherited the old family home from her grandmother. It had taken her a lot longer to sort herself out than she'd anticipated. Moving is always stressful and time consuming, and it wasn't that she'd underestimated the upheaval it would cause, only the state the place was in. Shabby curtains and carpets, rotten window and door frames was one thing, more or less what she'd expected, but having to replace most of the floor boards, all electric wiring, all plumbing and the roof, came as a shock. On top of that, Jane wanted to respect the past, the memories trapped within the walls of this ancestral residence which had belonged to her family for generations. So she was keen to preserve as many of the original features as possible, which, at times, proved a tremendous structural challenge, especially when it came to ensuring that the ceiling was properly supported to prevent it from collapsing. No matter how beautiful the original wooden beams looked, they were ripe to crumble at any moment, making it imperative to replace them. All in all, renovation was a serious undertaking, but definitely worth the expense and effort, and soon it would be finished, and she would have a most magnificent home – one she could never have afforded to buy, not even in its desolate state, let alone after renovations were completed.

Minford Hall was an impressive, albeit little known, country estate. The mansion itself was surrounded by a respectably sized walled garden, which kept it hidden from view to anybody travelling along the passing road. If it hadn't been for the multiple road signs announcing the entrance in 1000, 500, 300, 100 metres, Jane might have driven right past it. Legend has it that it was built by some unfaithful earl so he could entertain his concubines without his wife's knowledge.

It was a beautiful building with elegantly frescoed ceilings, although, apart from some paintings, the occasional ornate fire place, a chaise longue here and there, the rooms lacked the embellishment of furniture to render it truly interesting. As Jane walked into yet another empty room, she almost walked straight out again. But when she spotted the large mirror adorning one of the walls, her female vanity drew her inside with the intention to quickly check her make-up and hair, fearing that she might look somewhat dishevelled after running from the car park to the reception in the pouring rain. Yet, standing right opposite to what she had assumed was a mirror, she was surprised not to be confronted with her reflection. Instead, she discovered a faint silhouette of a young female right in the centre of the rather elaborate gilded frame. Instinctively she moved nearer the image. The closer she got, the clearer the image became, and as the features of the woman became more defined, Jane thought the person started to look weirdly familiar. Whilst the vision was by no means a reflection of herself, it certainly bore a strong resemblance to her. Not her as she was now, but a younger version of her – the long, untameable, flaming red hair, the voluptuous lips, the blue eyes, the ghostly pale complexion – just as Jane had looked when she was about eighteen. A look, by the way, she had hated and spent most of her life trying to defeat, although lots of people, particularly her parents, insisted she resembled a Pre-Raphaelite Beauty. The only thing defying the possibility that this might indeed be her was the style of clothing - she was certain she had never worn a baggy, purply-black gown, not even as fancy dress.

Jane felt that there was more to this vision than had so far been revealed to her. Whilst the woman's face with her pensive, sad look was now brought sharply into focus, the background was blurred, but seemed filled with mysteriousness as it changed from lighter to darker shades and the indistinguishable shapes, showing only outlines of another person and a building, appeared utterly disproportionate to the domineering figure in the foreground.

Jane stood there, still staring at this undeniable likeness, when a member of staff walked into the room to announce that only ten minutes remained before closing time. Getting no reaction, the woman advanced towards Jane whilst repeating her reminder about closing time.

'Oh,' replied Jane startled. 'I'm sorry I had completely lost myself in this extraordinary mirror-like painting.'

'Painting? Oh no, it is definitely a mirror,' retorted the woman, then added proudly, 'Quite a magnificent one, isn't it? A genuine 19th century specimen, the intricate woodwork is all hand carved and covered in thick gold leaf.'

As she took her place next to Jane, the mirror projected a true reflection of the two women in front of it. Gone were all traces of the Pre-Raphaelite beauty. Jane left Minford Hall dazed with confusion and doubting her senses.

She went back, however, the next day to find out whether she had but imagined the apparition previously. Her first delight about the discovery that she had not, soon gave way to serious concern. As Jane stood again rooted in front of the mirror, mesmerised by the familiar features of this young woman from a long-gone era, a vision that clearly had not presented itself to any of the staff, she started to worry about her sanity. She had never *seen* things before. Was she ill? Was she hallucinating? What could be the significance?

Jane spent the next few weeks visiting other Victorian mansions, planting herself in front of every mirror she could find but without any unusual occurrence. Eventually, she confided in a friend who, after accompanying Jane to visit the special mirror with the result of confirming Jane's previous experiences there, wherein the vision was only visible to herself, suggested she should research her family's history in case there was an ancestor linked with Minford Hall, which might be the cause for triggering such a strong reaction in Jane's mind. The research, however, unveiled no connection between Jane's family and Minford Hall. There was no evidence of any ancestor, not even a distantly related one, having been remotely associated with the neighbouring estate. Nor did she unearth any family secrets. Apart from the disappearance of what would have been her great-great-great aunt, more than a hundred years ago, her ancestors seemed to have led a rather unremarkable and uneventful life.

Jane returned many more times in defiance of the apparition but always left defeated by its obstinate recurrence. Plagued and frustrated, she decided to place an ad in one of the daily newspapers, headed *'Possible Impossibility'* inviting people who may, like herself, have ever looked in a mirror and beheld anything but their own reflection, to contact her via the advised post box address. Of course, her request returned an array of crazy replies – from harmless ghost stories to disgusting pornographic fantasies. Jane was on the verge of binning the remaining heap of letters when an envelope displaying the words *Minford Hall* written in red ink, caught her eye. The note inside read: *If you are referring to the mirror at Minford Hall, then we should meet.* There was no name, only a mobile phone number.

Two days later, Jane was on her way to Minford Hall to meet the man, who had so far insisted on staying nameless. She entered the reception area wondering how she might spot her mysterious rendezvous when a grey-haired man in his mid-fifties hurried towards her.

'You must be Jane,' he said whilst extending his hand.

'And you are?' she asked sounding slightly cross although she did shake his hand.

He apologised for not having introduced himself immediately but assured her that he would shortly explain everything, suggesting they should embark on a tour of the mansion where they would get more privacy than in the busy reception area. His name was William Archibald Minford, a descendant of the owner of this hall. He revealed to Jane all he knew about his lecherous ancestor who had not only entertained concubines in his secret hide-away, but also brought young innocent girls here to be seduced by him or his guests, depending on how he rated their beauty. Whether they came willingly, or were lured by some false pretences, or taken by force when spotted on a lonely afternoon walk, nobody knew. He then recounted his experience with that same mirror. In his case, the vision depicted his ancestor, to whom, he elaborated, he bore a remarkable resemblance, standing tall and imposing in the courtyard of a disproportionately small Minford Hall. He carried on to explain that, due to the presence of some hovering shadows, he had always felt there was more to the image than he was able to see, that there was another part belonging to this apparition which his mind was unable to conjure up.

After listening to Jane relating her encounter with the mirror and the mention of her ancestor's disappearance, William Archibald Minford seemed most excited, declaring that he was convinced that they each provided the other's missing piece of the image and that he had hoped, for countless years now, for some occurrence that might help him solve the mystery by adding the missing pieces to this ancient puzzle. The two descendants, both look-alikes of their respective ancestors, conceded however, that their visions may not merge but agreed nonetheless that it was well worth the experiment. So, expecting nothing but hoping for everything, they stepped in front of the mirror.

Within seconds, Minford Hall appeared in all its past glory before being banished to the background by the beautiful young, red-haired maiden with luscious lips and ivory complexion. But as the on-lookers feasted on her beauty, a dark shadow arose behind her which swiftly transformed into the threatening image of Earl William Archibald Minford, the first, Lord of the Manor. Although noticeably terrified by his appearance, the young girl stood proud and in defiance. When his hands closed on her neck, she offered no resistance. Death, untimely though it was, was preferable to the alternative.

Strictly, as this virginal beauty began to sink to the floor, the image changed one last time. The earl, not his victim, disappeared. An insignificant Minford Hall was left in the background, towered over by the green hills of its surroundings until, at last, they were both out-done by the victory of purity as the young Pre-Raphaelite beauty positioned herself triumphantly, leaning on a balustrade and looking on in a mood of sad contemplation, took centre stage.

A short while later, the girl too had vanished from the centre of the mirror, leaving Jane and William to face only their own reflections.

141

www.ingramcontent.com/pod-product-compliance
Lightning Source LLC
Chambersburg PA
CBHW051120300726
48981CB00021B/490/J